William H. Weber

Last Stand: Turning the Tide

Alamo Publishing

Alamo Publishing

ISBN: 978-1-926456-06-5

Cover design: Keri Knutson

Dedication

First, a thank you to the early readers who were kind enough to comment on early drafts of the manuscript. In no particular order, John Alex Groff, H. Rossi, Stephen Myers, LBC and Gary Stevens. Each of you was invaluable in helping to shape this book.

To my wife and family for always being there. And finally to the fans who make it all worthwhile.

Last Stand: Turning the Tide

In spite of Oneida's heroic stand against the Chinese, foreign armies are poised along the foothills of the Appalachian Mountains, preparing for the final assault. America's defeat is inevitable. For John, turning the tide will mean going deep behind enemy lines and organizing the sort of insurgency he fought so hard against in Iraq. But more than that, it'll mean coming to terms with the brutality of war and the realization that sometimes the deepest scars are the ones that can't be seen.

Recap of Last Stand Books 1-3

When an EMP plunges the country into darkness, John Mack decides to use his military training to help his neighbors deal with the crisis. Their difficulties soon worsen when they become targeted by a ruthless gang of criminals, leaving John to prepare those around him to fight a battle they can't possibly win. The resulting carnage leaves the streets of Willow Creek devastated.

After fleeing to his cabin in northern Tennessee, John discovers that a tyrant named The Chairman has taken hold of the local town of Oneida. His home goes up in flames and his loved ones are kidnapped.

His path of vengeance leads him to a group of Patriots, many of whom have also suffered at the hands of The Chairman. Together they storm Oneida and end The Chairman's reign of terror.

Everything they thought they knew changes when they learn that the EMP was only the opening salvo of a larger invasion plan and that the armies of Russia, China and North Korea are poised to push across the Mississippi River in order to complete their conquest.

Standing in their way is the tiny town of Oneida. Together with the help of disparate elements of surviving US forces, they just manage to hold on. Bypassed by a frustrated enemy, Oneida becomes a symbol of resistance as the stage becomes set for the final battle which will decide whether America will remain forever free or live in tyranny.

From the Author

The late bestselling author Elmore Leonard once said: "When you write, try to leave out all the parts readers skip." Dutch's words rang loudly in my ears as I sat down to tackle the Last Stand series. My goal was always to tell an educational and entertaining tale. To say that I've been surprised by the reception the series has received would be a massive understatement. Even more astonishing has been the support and well-wishes from readers all over the world. It's been a great ride so far. Thank you again for joining me. And know that although the Last Stand series is coming to an end, this is only the beginning.

William H. Weber

Quick Reference

Abbreviations

APC: Armored Personnel Carrier
GPS: Global Positioning System
HE: High Explosive
IED: Improvised Explosive Device
IFV: Infantry Fighting Vehicle
KIA: Killed in Action
JTAC: Joint Terminal Attack Controller
MBT: Main Battle Tank

Characters

Colonel Higgs: Frontline commander
Colonel Guo Fenghui: Aide to General Liang
Colonel Li Keqiang: Head of Chinese Military Intelligence
Devon: Young security guy
David Newbury: Concentration camp survivor
Dixon: Soldier at the front
General Brooks: Head of forces in Oneida
General Dempsey: Chairman of the Joint Chiefs of Staff
General Wei Liang: The supreme commander of all Chinese and North Korean forces
Heller: Explosives expert
Henry: Ham radio operator
Huan Wei: Chinese prisoner of war
Jang Yong-ho: Camp Commandant
Jerry Fowler: Former employee at Y-12
Moss: Head of security

Ray Gruber: Vice Mayor of Oneida
Robert Rodriguez: Electronics specialist/radio operator
Zhang Shuhong: Chinese special forces commander

Vehicles and Weapons

American:

A-10 Warthog: Tank-destroying plane
Ac-130: Ground attack aircraft
Abrams M1A2: Main battle tank
AH-64 Apache: Attack helicopter
AT-4: Disposable anti-tank weapon
Barrett M82: .50 cal sniper rifle
Bradley: M2 Bradley Fighting Vehicle
F-22 Raptor: Fighter jet
Javelin: Fire-and-forget anti-tank missile
Remington 700: Sniper rifle used by Reese
M249: Light machine gun
M4 Carbine: Assault rifle
SAW: Squad automatic weapon (light machine gun)

Chinese:

QBZ-03: Assault rifle
Type 77: Officers pistol
ZBD-08: Infantry fighting vehicle

Russian:

AK-47/74: Assault rifle
BTR-T: Infantry fighting vehicle
Mil Mi-28 Havoc: Attack helicopter

RPG: Rocket-propelled grenade
Sukhoi Su-27: Fighter jet
T-90: Russian main battle tank
TOS-1: Mobile rocket artillery

Chapter 1

The early-morning sun warmed John's face as he listened to the caged pigeons cooing next to him. He was trying to process a million jumbled thoughts at once.

Oneida's streets and buildings still bore the deep scars of battle. Burned-out vehicles and piles of rubble clogged the entire length of Alberta Street. The enemy dead had been thrown unceremoniously into a mass grave, weapons and equipment salvaged for later use. Even though the Chinese troops had backed away, the loose ring around the town served as a constant reminder that another attack could happen at any time. Next to him Wilbur Powel was talking, his words muffled and distant.

"They've been used for at least a couple thousand years," Wilbur was saying. An older man with wire-rimmed glasses and a bad combover, he'd once run a small insurance company in Oneida. That was, before the EMP.

"What's been used?" John asked.

"Carrier pigeons. I was saying they've been used for centuries. Way back to the ancient Persians."

Oneida was observing strict radio silence before the mission to the Y-12 National Security Complex in Oak Ridge. Any information going to or from the town would either need to be sent over land by messenger—a risk that was far too great given that PLA troops still encircled the city—or by carrier pigeons. That was where Wilbur came in.

"Used 'em in both World Wars. Fact, when the Germans caught on, they sent hawks up to hunt 'em down."

"What's this?" John asked, referring to a wire in the cage.

Wilbur glared in with his one good eye. "That's the signal wire, which rings a bell when a bird arrives with a message."

John smiled. "Sorta like email."

"I wouldn't know nothing about that," Wilbur spat. "Rotary phone and a typewriter were all I ever needed. Only good thing that came from that pulse bomb I suppose was that it fried the cell phones those teenagers are always staring at like zombies."

"You've got a point there," John said, unable to keep from thinking about Gregory, nor feeling the sting that came along with not having freed his son. "So where can we send them?" John asked.

Wilbur stared up at the sky and pursed his lips. "Least half my birds were killed when a Chinese shell landed nearby. I do got one group that can travel as far as Greensboro."

"That's too far. We need something closer to the front lines."

"Then it'll have to be Boone, North Carolina. Just a stone's throw from the Appalachians. I got five birds who used to make that trip on a regular basis."

John nodded, folding his arms. "That should do. But it'll mean including instructions to deliver the message to General Dempsey." He was mostly talking to himself. "All right, once we've returned, either Henry or Rodriguez will come by with the message."

"What's it gonna say?" Wilbur asked, although the doubtful expression on his face made it clear he didn't expect to be told.

"I wish I could tell you," John said apologetically.

"But with Phoenix on the loose, we can't take any chances. Until we can figure the traitor is, we'll be making quite a bit of use out of these birds of yours."

"Then you'll need to post guards near them cages," Wilbur said.

John nodded. The old man was right. If Phoenix was on the lookout for targets of opportunity, cutting off their communication with the outside world would be a major setback.

Although John couldn't divulge the details to Wilbur, the message they'd eventually send to General Dempsey would detail the success or failure of the mission to Y-12. The former would hopefully signal a green light to begin preparations for a large-scale counterattack. The latter would likely mean that John was dead.

Moss arrived a moment later driving an old, beat-up golf cart. He pulled to a stop and nodded at Wilbur. "Hate to break up your fun, boss, but they're ready for you."

He was referring to the team going to Y-12 and the plane that would get them there. John climbed on board the golf cart, not entirely able to squash that sinking feeling that he might never return.

Chapter 2

Cutting through the back roads, which weren't nearly so cluttered with debris, they arrived in the center of town within minutes. There they met up with Jerry Fowler, Reese and the armed escort that would bring them to Scott Municipal Airport. Located a couple miles southwest of town, the airport was well within Oneida's zone of control and because of its short runway had largely been ignored by the Chinese during their failed attempt to overrun the town. Still, in spite of its good luck, the airport hadn't gone completely unscathed. At one point during the battle, a shell had landed near the hangar, destroying two small planes and damaging another. But the decades-old four-seat Cessna 172 Skyhawk designated to fly them south to Oak Ridge was undamaged.

"Aren't you gonna say goodbye to Diane and Emma?" Moss asked, still sporting the woodland fatigues and multicolored mohawk he'd worn during the battle. He hadn't changed in days, and by the odor wafting off of him, he hadn't washed either.

"The only thing it'll do is worry them more," John replied. His gear was waiting for him at the rendezvous point and he began to put it on. "When she asks where I am, you tell her I've gone away on business."

"Oh, yeah," Moss cackled. "She's gonna love that. In case you've forgotten, she and I aren't on the best terms right now."

Dimples formed as he gave his head of security a

wink. "I thought you were a glutton for punishment, Moss? Besides, it'll be a good opportunity to work on your diplomacy skills. You do intend to be mayor someday, don't you?"

"I don't intend to live that long."

Once he was geared up, John went to greet Jerry and Reese. Jerry was decked out in a green aviator's jumpsuit, his belly showing prominently. He looked nervous and rightly so. When they'd first met, Jerry had survived a vicious assault in the Home Depot where he'd been tied to a shower and left for dead. From there he'd been thrust into probably the most intense urban combat John had seen since his days in Iraq. So much for bad luck.

Reese stood casually beside him, puffing on a Chinese cigarette he'd likely taken off a dead Commie soldier. John waved his hand in front of his face. "Put that thing out before we all die of cancer."

Smiling, Reese complied, stubbing it out with the toe of his boot. Slung over his back was a new gift he'd received from General Brooks—a Barrett M82 .50 caliber sniper rifle—and hanging from a two-point sling was an M4.

Reese motioned with the assault rifle. "She belonged to Captain Bishop," he said solemnly. "After he got chewed up by that Commie AA gun, I figured I'd bring her along and see if I couldn't win him a little payback."

"Quick in and quick out," John told the sniper. "I don't need to tell you the best missions are the ones where you never fire a shot."

"That may be," Reese replied. "But they sure aren't the most gratifying."

This kind of talk was making Jerry look about as white as a sheet. John was quick to change the subject. "You have everything you need, Jerry?"

Jerry nodded. His beard had crumbs in it.

"You eat this morning?" John asked.

"A little," Jerry said, glancing down at his belly self-consciously.

"Well, just make sure you keep it down when we're in the air." John glanced around. "Speaking of air, where's the pilot?"

"At the airport, getting the plane ready," Reese told him as he pulled out another cigarette and clamped it between his teeth. He was barely done when he caught the change in John's expression. "Don't worry, Colonel. I won't light it up. I'm saving it that for when we get back."

If they ever got back, John thought, but didn't say.

They'd briefed the mission late into the previous night, going over every eventuality and working in fail-safes and redundancies at every turn. When embarking on a mission, it wasn't good enough to have a single plan. You needed options for when things inevitably went wrong. General Dempsey had assured them that once they reached Oak Ridge soldiers from the 3rd Infantry Division as well as scientists from the research facility would greet them. After that it was a question of rigging the warhead to a balloon and sending it high into the atmosphere.

And with that they clambered into the Humvees and headed for the airport. Despite the short distance, two Bradley Fighting Vehicles were assigned to escort them. John peered out at Moss from the passenger window as they pulled away, watching his head of security standing at attention.

Chapter 3

When they arrived minutes later, John exited the Humvee to the sound of distant gunfire.

"Sounds like a skirmish north of town," Reese said.

Ever since the recent Chinese push into the area, small skirmishes had been going on along most of the perimeter as the Communists looked for weak spots. At least that was what the Chinese wanted them to think. The truth was the bulk of their forces had moved east as part of the buildup against the American position along the Appalachian Mountains. What had been left behind was intended to keep the units defending Oneida contained. A reality which was going to make the pilot's job a tricky one.

John spotted the pilot by the plane, tinkering with the engine. But it was the paint job on the aircraft that really caught his attention. A red stripe and Communist star ran along the fuselage. It had been redone to look like something from the Chinese Air Force. The hope was any foreign troops would hesitate a few precious seconds before firing. General Dempsey had also been informed so they weren't shot down by the American soldiers protecting Oak Ridge.

John and the other two members of the team headed in that direction while the soldiers protecting them fanned out to guard the perimeter.

"You the pilot?" John asked.

The man set his wrench down. "Billy Ray Bryant, at

your service," he said, flashing a set of gleaming white teeth. He was a large man, over two hundred pounds, with forearms the size of some men's legs. His tanned face was round and covered with a patchwork of curly facial hair.

"Why weren't you at the rendezvous point in town?" John asked him, eager to get on with the mission, but just as eager to get a sense of the man who was about to fly them into danger. "Right now you're the only pilot we have. Coming out here without an escort could have gotten you killed and jeopardized everything we're about to do."

Billy Ray pulled a hanky from his back pocket and wiped the grease from his hands. "You want my plane to run, don't you?" he shot back. "I already need to put up with the fact that she's been painted to look like the enemy. Besides, I been here since dawn making sure she won't dump us the first chance she gets. These machines are like women, you gotta treat 'em nice or they'll turn on you something fierce."

John fought the urge to smile at the man's eccentricity. "Will she fly or not?"

"Oh, she'll fly," Billy Ray said, slamming the engine compartment shut and motioning dramatically. "After you, gentlemen."

•••

The Cessna pointed her nose into the wind as Billy Ray thrust the throttle forward. All four men were pushed back in their seats as the tiny plane lurched forward, its engines rumbling.

"We got a heavy load," Billy Ray said. "But we should make it into the air just fine."

Ahead of them was a stretch of runway which ended at a treeline.

"What do you mean 'should?'" John said, concerned.

"Just hold on tight," the pilot replied as the plane reached its full speed and he pulled back on the stick with both hands.

The small craft shook as the nose lifted off the ground and the runway slowly disappeared from view.

"Come on, baby," Billy Ray pleaded. "Don't treat me like this." His arms shook as he yanked on the controls.

Slowly, the rest of the plane released its hold on the earth and they skimmed over the top of the trees with barely inches to spare.

In the back, Jerry looked positively terrified. His hands gripped the edges of the seat, and he wore the smile of a man on a violent rollercoaster. Next to him Reese was fast asleep.

Sweat trailed from Billy Ray's brow. He let out a whoop. "I knew she wouldn't let me down."

The tops of trees flickered beneath them as they sped along only meters from the ground. Flying fast and low was intended to avoid any Chinese air batteries. Just like the one John spotted in a clearing up ahead. Communist troops were camped out in a field. As they flew over, a few raised their weapons, but didn't fire.

A second later they passed out of sight.

"Looks like the paint job worked," John said, glancing back.

Billy Ray nodded. "Heading there is one thing. Coming back might be something else entirely. It's like that old saying goes. 'Fool me once, shame on you. Fool me twice, shame on me.'"

"Our enemy isn't nearly as dumb as we wish he were," John said.

"You're right about that, Colonel. Just look at the mess we're in. Most of what used to be ours is now theirs and it seems like the little bit we have left keeps getting smaller."

"They're on a winning streak, no doubt, but it can't go on forever. If we get this right, the shoe might soon be on the other foot."

Billy Ray peered over at him, one eyebrow cocked. "You sure are optimistic. Most of the folks in town these last few days are pretty much doom and gloom. They say it's just a matter of time before we're all talking Mandarin."

John stared out the window, watching the horizon as the Cessna pushed forward. "It's difficult to blame them, I suppose. Many are still in shock."

"Shocked that we been attacked?"

"More so that we might lose. Think about it. The last two major wars we fought were against enemies that couldn't stand toe to toe with us on the battlefield. I suppose it was only a question of time before someone figured out a way to turn our greatest strength into our greatest weakness."

"You mean our freedom?"

John laughed. "No, our technology. In the *Odyssey*, the only way Ulysses and his men could defeat the giant Cyclops was by gouging his eye out. We've been blinded, but now it's our turn to return the favor."

They crossed the New River and John knew they were only a few miles from their destination. He began rechecking his gear.

A sticker of the Alaskan state flag sat above the control panel facing Billy Ray and it caught John's attention. "That where you're from?"

"Alaska? Nah, just a place I worked for a while, running rich corporate types up to remote fishing lodges. Most of 'em didn't have a clue what they were doing, much less how to survive if things ever took a turn for the worst. Felt more like a glorified chauffeur for a bunch of schoolkids most of the time. But let me tell you, pushing that deep into the brush can get your heart racing at times. Make one mistake out there and you just became someone's dinner."

"I see," John said. "You one of those adrenaline junkies?"

Billy Ray let out a hearty laugh. "You might say that. But my addiction, if you can call it that, used to be a lot worse. Trust me when I tell you bush runs in Alaska ain't nothing compared to flying drugs up from Columbia."

John's ears perked up.

"Yup, that's usually the reaction I get from folks. You don't need to do it more than a handful of times to know it just ain't worth it, regardless of how much money those kingpins throw at you. So, yeah, I've done my fair share of evasive flying, if that's what you were getting at."

"I'm hoping there won't be a need to test you on that," John said, spotting a collection of buildings in the distance ranged along a runway.

"There she is," Billy Ray said, pointing one of his meaty fingers toward Oak Ridge. He nudged the nose down a few degrees.

John reached back and shook Reese awake.

"We're on in five."

Chapter 4

The Y-12 National Security Complex was a sprawling set of structures located in a lush valley. As they lined up with the runway, John could see lots of activity on the ground. Men in fatigues loaded crates onto an old steam train while nearby other soldiers stood guard. While their plane was still a few hundred feet off the ground, anti-aircraft emplacements came into view. There were several of them, positioned in and around a number of buildings which had already been damaged during previous attacks.

General Dempsey had informed John that the 3rd Infantry Division was holding the approaches from the north and the west. But holding was a relative term. From up here, it didn't appear the tiny figures scrambling below seemed all that intent on staying. On the contrary, they appeared to be withdrawing anything and everything they could lay their hands on. If John was right, then whatever was left behind would likely be destroyed in order to prevent it from falling into enemy hands.

The Cessna touched down with a thump and Jerry let out a yelp. The sound made Reese and the others laugh, especially Billy Ray, whose belly gyrated. Once on the ground, they didn't need to taxi very far before a group of Humvees came into view, each with a gunner manning a .50 caliber machine gun.

The military vehicles skidded to a stop and soldiers poured out just as John and the others exited the plane.

An imposing black officer in blue and gray fatigues stepped forward. "Colonel Mack?"

"Yes," John replied as the two men shared a salute. The name on his chest read Porter and the insignia next to that indicated he was a colonel. Beside him was a red-haired, clean-cut civilian in a white lab coat.

"This is Sean Murphy," Colonel Porter said. "He's with the Nuclear Emergency Support Team. We've set aside a decommissioned W-89 two-hundred-kiloton nuclear warhead for you at the Uranium Processing Facility."

"We appreciate the help, Colonel," John told him, noting the stern expression on the officer's face. "Looks like you've got your hands full."

"Well, to be frank, you couldn't have picked a worse time. When word came down from General Dempsey what you folks were planning, I told him it was downright crazy."

John smiled. "You wouldn't be the first."

"I may not, but let me be clear about something. When that train is fully loaded, me and my men are leaving this place and blowing it sky-high whether your mission is completed or not."

"I understand," John replied.

"I'm also leaving you with two of my men, Fuller and Lambert. This is a large complex. Anything you need, they'll get it for you."

John thanked him.

"Is there anything else you need before I go?" Colonel Porter asked.

Reese stepped forward. "How about a pack of Marlboro?"

Porter threw John a look. "How about some caviar and a box of Cubans?"

"Don't worry, Colonel," John said, elbowing Reese. "We'll get out of your hair now."

"Hey, he asked," Reese said.

Porter disappeared into one of the Humvees and peeled away.

"Never mind that now," John said as he turned to Jerry. "Take Fuller and Lambert to help you prep the balloons. I'm not sure how many you'll need, but this warhead's gonna weigh at least a couple hundred pounds."

Next to him, Sean Murphy checked the clipboard he was holding. "Three hundred and twenty-four, to be exact."

"I figure that's three or four three-thousand-gram balloons," Jerry said, starting to calm down now that he was back in his element. "Finding the balloons and helium shouldn't be an issue. I'm just worried we might be short on time. If the Chinese start to—"

"You let the 3rd Infantry Division worry about the Chinese," John cut him off. "You just get those balloons ready."

The men all headed for the two Humvees after that: Jerry and the two soldiers in one, John, Reese and Sean Murphy in the other. Billy Ray came running up.

"What about me? What should I do?"

"You guard the plane," John told him.

"But I don't have a gun. I need some firepower, man."

"With arms like that?" Reese said. "Heck, you don't need a gun."

The Humvees tore off after that, leaving Billy Ray looking down at his biceps, nodding with approval.

Chapter 5

The Uranium Processing Facility was a new-looking building and one Murphy told them had been part of the complex's recent overhaul. He led them by flashlight to a concrete room with a high ceiling. Stacks all around them held missiles and bombs.

Reese whistled. "A direct hit on this place and they'll be scraping up what's left of you with a spatula."

"If you're lucky," Murphy shot back. He pointed to a bomb rack where the W-89 was laid out. A small compartment stood open with wires hanging out. "I've already begun to prep the warhead, but I wasn't sure how you wanted to set the timer."

"We need as much altitude as possible," John told him. "Jerry thinks he might be able to get it as high as thirty miles."

Murphy scratched his chin. "Then a regular timer may be a problem. What if the ascent is quicker than we expect? Or worse, what if it's slower? The warhead could detonate at the wrong altitude."

"What about hooking it up to an altimeter?" Reese offered, not taking his own suggestion very seriously.

"That isn't a horrible idea," Murphy said. "We could set it to explode when it reaches the thirty-mile mark."

"I'm sure Jerry should have something we can use," John said. "We'll also need to find some kind of cradle to rig the warhead to the balloon. Reese and I will go secure that altimeter while you find us that cradle. We'll meet back here in fifteen minutes."

John and Reese double-timed it from the processing facility to the Humvee outside. Thick cumulonimbus clouds were rolling in from the east. They were white and fluffy like the cumulus clouds most people were familiar with, except these ones reached up to five miles into the atmosphere.

Within minutes they caught up with Jerry and the two soldiers, wrestling large canisters of helium into the release zone. As the former Y-12 meteorologist had taken great pains to explain to them, it was imperative that the latex balloons themselves not be torn or otherwise compromised during this delicate procedure.

"We need one of your altimeters," John said.

Jerry stood up straight, arching his back. Sweat ran down the sides of his face and his hair was matted to his head. "Altimeter? I don't have one. Our instrumentation normally records atmospheric pressure, temperature, humidity and wind speed."

Reese swore. "Maybe we just take our chances on the timer then."

John shook his head. This was a textbook example of how any operation, no matter how well planned, could be stopped dead in its tracks by the tiniest obstacle. He'd been so worried about procuring the warhead and arriving in one piece he hadn't considered how they would determine the optimal altitude for detonation. This was the reason redundancy was so ingrained in a soldier's mind. But more than that, it was the importance of quick, creative thinking.

An image of Billy Ray's round, bearded face rose up before John's inner eye.

"We'll use the one from the Cessna," John shouted, clapping his hands together.

The others looked surprised.

"Will that work?" Reese asked.

"It'll have to."

Minutes later they found Billy Ray, sitting in the Skyhawk's cockpit. Nearby, soldiers hustled as they continued to load crates with nuclear symbols onto the train.

"We need something from your plane," John told him.

Billy Ray sat up quickly. "Excuse me?"

"I need your altimeter and fast. The entire mission depends on it."

Billy Ray's lips formed a perfect O for a moment. Before he could answer, a rumbling noise in the distance caught their attention. Then on the back of that came another sound as the air-raid sirens burst into life. Soldiers ran for cover. Those manning the anti-aircraft defenses cinched up their helmets.

Two Chinese Sukhoi Su-27 fighters streaked by, engaging afterburners as ground-to-air missiles lifted off after them. Quickly, they banked right and released flares to fool the oncoming missiles.

Reese rolled up his sleeves. "Looks like we just ran out of time."

Chapter 6

They reached the Uranium Processing Facility as another bomb exploded somewhere nearby, shaking the ground.

"Old Billy Ray wasn't too happy we gutted part of his control panel," Reese said.

"Maybe not," John told him. "But I just hope he takes my advice and finds some cover for that plane. That's our ride home."

Murphy was splicing wires when the two men arrived, altimeter in hand.

"Did you find that cradle?" John asked, in no mood to hear they had another problem.

"This was the best I could find," Murphy replied, pointing to the screw pin shackle.

Another explosion rocked the building.

"Those bombs are getting closer," John said, worried. He handed the altimeter to Murphy, who got to work connecting it and setting the detonator to go off at a hundred and sixty thousand feet.

Once that was done, the three men pushed the rack the warhead was resting on over to the Humvee and loaded it in using the winch.

"I won't arm it until the last minute," Murphy said. They'd be out in the open with a nuclear warhead while Chinese fighters were busy dropping bombs on their heads.

The pungent smell of cordite was thick in the air outside as they struggled to move the heavy warhead toward the Humvee's rear door.

Nearby a pile of aircraft wreckage burned on the ground near the Y-12 salvage yard.

"Looks like they got them," John said as the air-raid sirens stopped.

Reese smiled. "Lady Luck is smiling on us, I can feel it."

"Don't jinx it," John shot back.

The three of them finished loading the warhead, hopped into the vehicle and headed for Jerry and his balloons.

They'd turned a corner onto the runway when three enormous translucent spheres came into view.

As they arrived, John could see that even Jerry looked hopeful. John sprang out. "Are we ready to launch?" he asked.

"Almost," Jerry said, wiping sweat from his brow. "Only one more balloon to go."

The soldiers with him also looked anxious. Just then the radio on Lambert's belt went off.

"Private Lambert, this is Colonel Porter. I need you and Fuller back at headquarters right away." The strain in Porter's voice was obvious even to John, who'd only just met the man.

"Yes, sir," Lambert replied. "On the double."

"What's going on?" John asked. "Is the train about to leave?"

"No clue, sir."

John held out his hand. "Let me have your radio a moment."

"Sir?"

"Your radio, give it to me."

The soldier did as he was told.

"Colonel Porter, this is John…"

"Colonel Mack," Porter shot back, "I suggest you and your friends finish what you came here to do because we've got a whole Chinese division heading your way."

John's pulse quickened. "The defensive perimeter's been breached?"

"Breached? It's been annihilated. We're pushing out of here in ten minutes. I suggest you do the same."

"What about our air cover?"

"I'll hold on as long as I can, but I'm not interested in leaving any of my men behind."

John tried not to let the others see the worry on his face.

Then came the thunder of more jets streaking in from the west and John's concern wasn't only for the mission. He was beginning to wonder if they'd make it out of here alive.

Chapter 7

The air-raid sirens began blaring again as John and Murphy helped Jerry fill the final weather balloon.

"Reese," John called out. "Find Billy Ray and tell him to get the Cessna ready."

"With those things flying around?"

Almost in response, AA fire erupted from the roofs of the nearby buildings.

"Just do it."

Hopping into the Humvee, Reese sped away, heading for the airplane hangar where Billy Ray had sheltered the Cessna.

The balloons were attached to wire cables that were in turn connected to a stainless-steel ring jutting up from the ground. This was the same place from which Jerry had launched countless balloons in the past, although John was sure he'd never sent this kind of payload aloft.

A giant explosion nearly knocked them off their feet as the Uranium Processing Facility went up in a massive fireball.

"Once we get this warhead attached," John told Murphy, "I suggest you make a beeline for that train." Bristling with anti-aircraft defenses, the locomotive was the scientist's best chance of escape.

Murphy didn't argue.

"All right, let's finish this."

The three men seated the warhead into the cradle and secured the cables to each of the shackles. The procedure was similar to the way a Chinook helicopter used a towing cable to move vehicles and heavy artillery.

"How much longer on that balloon?" John shouted. Already in the distance was the sound of Chinese tanks engaging Porter's forces on the complex's perimeter.

"Almost there," Jerry replied.

John knelt beside the warhead. "All right, let's arm this thing."

Murphy nodded and went ahead. The sound of battle nearby was growing louder. Just then Reese appeared.

"Billy Ray and the Cessna should be here any minute."

John tried to control his breathing. This was when they were at their most vulnerable.

"I think it's time you catch that train," he told Murphy, whose red hair and pale skin were smeared with streaks of grease and dirt.

Murphy held out a hand and John shook it. "Good luck."

John nodded. "Give General Dempsey our best."

The scientist got into the Humvee and sped away right as the final balloon was completed.

"I hope you boys said your prayers this morning," John told them, his hand on the release.

Reese grinned while Jerry stood stiffly, sweating like a hog, his lips slightly parted as he glared at John's index finger.

"Here goes nothing." John released the clasp. A clang rang out as it let loose and the balloons jerked into the air, lifting the warhead beneath it. All three men watched it rise, heading for the thick cloud cover. Once there, it would be safe from the enemy fighters circling around.

The AA guns continued to spray streaks of fire into the sky. Beneath that came another sound, one they'd become all too familiar with. Billy Ray's Cessna. The plane emerged from behind a row of buildings, pushing toward the runway. Reese was still watching the balloon rise when an artillery shell struck a nearby water tower. Three hundred yards away, the silhouettes of enemy troops appeared. Soon rounds were impacting all around them.

"That's our cue," John said, gathering Jerry and Reese together and ushering them toward the Cessna. He grabbed Jerry's arm to pull him forward right as the man's legs gave out. More bullets dinged off the storage shed as they hit the ground. With chaos all around him, John struggled to assess whether Jerry had been hit. Then John found a small hole in his shirt and an exit wound in his back the size of a child's fist. It had severed his spine, killing him instantly. Jerry's eyes were still open and John closed them.

Reese looked over.

"He's dead." John scanned over to where the fire had come from and found at least a platoon-size group heading their way. "Buy us some time," John told Reese.

"That's the most sensible thing you've said all day," Reese quipped, swinging his Barrett around and flipping up the lens covers.

He dropped to the ground, estimating the enemy's range at around three hundred yards. With a few careful clicks he adjusted his scope and set to work.

The first shot hit the target's shoulder and took his arm off. He made another tweak, adjusting for wind speed, found his next target, steadied his breath and squeezed. The rifle cracked and jerked back as a Chinese soldier three hundred meters out was struck an inch below his throat.

"Most folks think snipers go for headshots, but most of the time that isn't necessary. Especially when you're firing a .50 cal round. Personally, I aim for the sternum." He fired twice more, killing both targets. "The real problem with a Barrett no one likes to talk about is that it kicks up a ton of dust. Risks giving away your position." An enemy poked his head around the edge of the groundwater treatment facility. "I see you, little buddy," Reese said, sending a round in his face. "That was a headshot, but see, I didn't have a choice."

Billy Ray was close enough now and John tapped Reese. "Enough showboating," John said sternly. "Time to move."

A few well-placed shots could often have a devastating effect on enemy morale, especially when they weren't sure where the fire was coming from or couldn't match its surgical accuracy.

Reese clambered up and grabbed his rifle as both men sprinted for the Cessna. Thankfully, a handful of buildings blocked their escape, but if the Chinese began flanking them, they might be caught out in the open.

Billy Ray had the Cessna pointed into the wind, away from the incoming Chinese troops. The pilot leaned over and opened the passenger door for John.

"You like to cut it close, don't you?"

"Did you miss us?" John asked, climbing aboard.

"I thought I was gonna have to hop on that train," Billy Ray said, checking to make sure both men were in. "Where's Jerry?"

John shook his head.

Billy Ray buried the throttle. "That's a real shame," he said. "Didn't know him more than a couple hours, but already I could tell he was a good guy." Buildings sped by as they picked up speed and lifted off, careful to keep low and away from the anti-aircraft fire. Below them, the AA crews on the buildings were leaving their positions and running for the train as it slowly began pulling away.

The plane banked left, toward Oneida, toward home, and John glanced back just in time to see the balloon disappear into the clouds.

"So, Colonel," Reese said, that unlit cigarette back between his teeth. "What are the odds this crazy plan of yours is gonna work?"

John gritted his teeth. Rising at a thousand feet per minute, the balloon would reach the optimum altitude in a little over two and a half hours. But it wasn't a question of whether he wanted the plan to work. The fate of the country depended on it.

Chapter 8

Not long after John and the others fled from Oak Ridge, the Supreme Commander of Chinese and North Korean forces, General Wei Liang, was attending his mid-afternoon briefing on the war's progress.

Tall and broad-faced, General Liang struck an imposing figure. It didn't matter that he preferred to keep his military hat on to hide his bald head, a condition far less common in Asia than it was in the Western world. Nor did it matter that the few scraps of hair he had left had long ago gone from a dusty grey to pearl white.

His current field headquarters was a humble series of buildings at Berry Field Air National Guard Base near Nashville. General Liang had come from an equally humble background. The son of a poor carpenter, and one of four siblings, he'd started out on the bottom rung. Now, at the ripe old age of sixty-four, he'd spent a lifetime clawing his way through the PLA ranks, waging far more battles against his political rivals than actual military engagements.

His ethnic Han background had helped open a few doors, no doubt. But being able to trace his roots back to the third-century-B.C. Han dynasty had only greased the wheels for his entry into the Xinyang Infantry School. A major-general before he was fifty, he'd led the 20th Army to enforce martial law in Beijing to suppress the Tiananmen Square protests.

His best years still lay ahead of him. When what remained of the United States was at last conquered, he would be installed as military governor, not unlike Dwight D. Eisenhower after Germany's defeat following World War II.

Although his reverence for Western military leaders seemed odd to some in the Communist Party, General Liang was quick to point out that the PLA itself was largely modeled after the United States' armed forces. Perhaps the most striking area where they differed was the initiative and flexibility demonstrated by their American counterparts. Chinese soldiers were taught to follow orders without question. Western troops were given a greater range of freedom and input when it came to planning and implementing operations. The word 'why' was simply not in a Chinese or North Korean soldier's vocabulary. As a result, American battlefield commanders from generals down to squad leaders were able to assess an ever-changing environment and make decisions on the fly.

The recent stubborn resistance they'd encountered at a small town north of Knoxville called Oneida was a case in point. Units that had nearly been destroyed a few days prior had managed to reform and fend off multiple attacks. The EMP blast, launched secretly from a Chinese sub along the western US shoreline months before, might have crippled the enemy's command and control infrastructure along with their ability to coordinate troops, but many of the pockets of resistance they'd encountered on their push eastward had proved harder to defeat than expected.

Setbacks aside, China was closing in on its final objectives and that was exactly what Colonel Li Keqiang, head of military intelligence, was telling them in his briefing. The scale of their achievement still surprised General Liang. Like Japan in December of 1941, they'd managed to launch a sneak attack American military planners had been too arrogant to believe was even possible. But the EMP, spectacular as it was, had only been the first part of a well-coordinated attack. With the simultaneous destruction of US military satellites and missile silos as well as Washington itself, the Eastern Alliance had taken the bold step Japan had failed to more than seventy years before.

To the Western nations, an invasion of Taiwan would have been seen as a likely precursor to conflict with America and that was precisely why they'd decided to save that for after the sleeping giant was put to bed once and for all.

But Colonel Li Keqiang's cheerful briefing didn't address a far more serious concern—the current naval war being waged in the Pacific. Chinese codebreakers knew that when word of the EMP finally reached American fleets sailing around the world, some had sought shelter in allied ports in order to re-establish communication with home and determine the best strategic course of action. Others that were caught out in the open as they rushed back had been hit with nuclear weapons and destroyed.

By some unfortunate stroke of luck, the US 3rd and 7th Fleets happened to be in Sydney and Melbourne harbors respectively at the time and escaped the worst of it. According to Chinese intelligence reports, US liaisons at Pine Gap had quickly organized high-level talks with the governments of Australia and New Zealand. Both countries had thrown in, offering support and combat vessels in a bid to take back the Pacific. Thankfully for the Eastern Alliance, Russian counter-submarine warfare had meant only three nuclear missiles had been fired from the sea, destroying St Petersburg, Nanjing and Shanghai. That the capitals of all three Eastern Alliance nations had been spared was a testament to Russia's ability to intercept the US boomers in time. Thus the need to knock the United States out of the war as soon as possible. Once that was accomplished, the handful of her allies who'd rushed to her side would inevitably withdraw from the conflict.

General Liang's attention returned to his current surroundings. Generators around Berry Field provided power and lights for laptops and sensitive equipment brought over from China following the EMP strike. The screen of his laptop moved to the final PowerPoint slide as Colonel Li Keqiang ended his presentation with a quote.

If you know the enemy and know yourself, you need not fear the result of a hundred battles. If you know yourself but not the enemy, for every victory gained you will also suffer a defeat. If you know neither the enemy nor yourself, you will succumb in every battle.

"That's Sun Tzu," Colonel Guo Fenghui whispered in Liang's ear. He was a thin man with boundless energy who was the most competent of Liang's four aides.

"Keqiang sure likes to be poetic, doesn't he?" The general's mind was still on the struggle to maintain control of the Pacific. "We must begin increasing production in our slave labor camps. If our supply lines over the Pacific are severed, we could be in trouble. I've got a Cuban cigar in the desk drawer of my office I'm saving for the day we announce our victory and I intend to smoke it."

Guo Fenghui nodded thoughtfully. "I'm confident you will, sir. As for production, we can utilize captured equipment for now since production in the camps is only starting to come online—"

Suddenly the briefing room went dark. But it wasn't only the lights that had gone out. Every laptop in the room was also dead. Shortly after came the sound of a thunderous explosion. A breathless major charged into the conference room, flashlight in hand, telling them a transport plane coming in to land had just fallen from the sky. He kept mumbling about the blinding flash he'd seen on the horizon right as the electrical equipment had shorted.

General Wei Liang didn't need to hear any more to understand what was going on. The far-fetched American plan Phoenix had warned them about, the very one they'd tried to thwart by pushing up their attack on Oak Ridge, had somehow succeeded and the war raging in the Pacific was the least of his worries.

Chapter 9

A ragged line of American slave laborers trudged from the farmers' fields that lay adjacent to the North Korean concentration camp near Jonesboro. Guards, their AKs fixed with bayonets and at the ready, kept a watchful eye as the column made its way back to the razor-wire fence line.

Once they arrived, the metal gates would be opened, allowing them to enter. If anyone tried to run, they'd be shot dead, something Brandon had seen with his own eyes. A mother and her young daughter had tried to sprint for the drainage ditches that cut through each field like trenches on a First World War battlefield. In theory, once the slave labor force made its way back into the camp, the two would follow those ditches until they reached the St. Francis forest nearby.

One of the North Korean guards, a pug-faced man wearing a dark green uniform and a flat-topped cap, had leveled his AK and fired without a single warning. Two shots had broken the late-afternoon silence. Neither the woman nor the little girl had made a sound as they tumbled to the ground.

The pug-faced guard shouted something in Korean Brandon didn't understand, but the proud smile on his face said enough. He was bragging to his guard friends about his marksmanship and the sight made Brandon long for an AK of his own so he could put one into that ugly face.

That had happened days ago. Brandon couldn't say how many, since there was no real way to keep track. Once they'd began the back-breaking work they'd been sent here to perform—in this case cultivating crops for the North Korean and Chinese forces—hours, days and weeks began to lose their meaning. But after the murder of that woman and her daughter, Brandon had seen a host of similar atrocities, many too vile to mention. Without a doubt, his dreams would be haunted for years to come. If, that was, he ever managed to leave this place.

Those were the discordant thoughts flitting through Brandon's head when a flash of blinding light in the sky caught his attention. Many of the prisoners and guards stopped and watched it for a moment, many shielding their eyes. It seemed to hang there forever before gradually fading. What could that have been? Had Knoxville been hit with a nuke?

Another thing which tended to dull in this place was one's cardinal sense. It wasn't until he'd made himself a rudimentary sun compass that he'd realized home was in a completely different direction.

The process had been simple enough. First one planted an eighteen-inch stick in the ground. Then every ten to fifteen minutes, smaller sticks would mark the top of the shadow from the larger one as the sun slowly traversed the sky. After recording three or four points, a distinct east-west line would begin to appear. With the knowledge that the sun rose in the east and set in the west, it then became simple to get a rough sense of each compass point. Since then, he'd understood that beyond the St. Francis forest lay his family and home.

Next to Brandon as they stumbled back toward camp was an exhausted and even thinner-looking Gregory.

Shortly after arriving, they'd been processed by a series of rough camp guards, stripped of their clothing and given sturdy brown trousers and a matching tunic. They slept in long prisoner barracks filled with bunk beds stacked four high and maybe a hundred deep. No one bothered to count. When they did eat, it was generally a watery broth with cabbage leaves and rice. They ate everything they were given, no matter how vile, as well as the few dwindling plants Brandon managed to forage here and there when the guards weren't looking. With the labor they were doing on a daily basis, they weren't getting nearly enough calories. A few among them had already died from starvation. Others' skeletal forms struggled against the heavy fabric of the prison uniforms they wore. These, Brandon figured, must have been part of the first group sent to the camp when it was being built.

Like a funeral procession, they made their way through the gate and into the central courtyard, where they lined up for a head count. The North Koreans wanted to make sure no one escaped this place and Brandon was left to wonder what they feared more, losing manpower or word of their atrocities getting out.

The work group Brandon and Gregory were a part of consisted of five hundred prisoners who were all lined up in tight formation. Soon, other work groups joined them until the courtyard was full. Whatever this was about, it was big.

Before them was the camp commandant, Jang Yong-ho, short and round. It seemed as though the higher your rank in the North Korean army, the bigger your belly. He spoke in broken English to an American named Ellis Stone, a former small-town sheriff turned collaborator and perhaps the most hated man in the camps.

Even to Brandon, the idea of American prisoners guarding one another seemed especially cruel. Perhaps it had something to do with the language barrier or perhaps it was a lack of able-bodied guards. No one could say, but he remembered reading that the Nazis had done the same to the Jews in the concentration camps of Europe during World War II, so the sight, wretched as it was, wasn't entirely shocking.

Once Jang had finished, Ellis began to speak.

"Each and every one of you knows that the penalty for attempting to escape is death," he said. His silver hair was tucked beneath his green North Korean guard cap. Ellis and his deputies wore a prison uniform just like everyone else, except theirs had yellow stars drawn on their chests. "We've recently learned of a large-scale escape plan. The ringleaders were arrested and tried this morning and will shortly be executed."

Gregory and Brandon shared a frightened look. Could they be talking about the escape Dixon and his fellow soldiers had been planning? Brandon searched the crowd without finding his friend's face.

Within minutes, a group of twenty prisoners were led before Jang, black sacks pulled over their heads, their hands lashed behind their backs. The camp commandant spoke to Ellis, who passed on the message.

"Before you stand the accused. Eighteen men and two women."

Then one by one, a North Korean guard went before them and thrust his bayonet into their bellies. Their shrieks of pain filled Brandon's heart with horror. One of those men was Dixon, he was sure of it.

Once they were done, Ellis and his deputies began clearing away the bodies.

Another twenty were led out and suffered a similar fate. Gregory had watched the first group, unable to look away, but now his eyes were fixed on the ground, his

fingers in his ears so he wouldn't have to listen to the sound they made as they were gutted like pigs. Brandon wanted to do the same, but the thought of losing Dixon kept him focused on the faceless prisoners. He was searching each of them for any kind of sign that would identify one of them as his friend.

A tug on Brandon's tunic startled him. He turned and nearly cried out when he saw Dixon, standing by his left shoulder.

"Keep your cool, kid," Dixon told him. "And do like Gregory here and avert your eyes. They're trying to get into our heads and break us from the inside out. Don't give them the satisfaction."

"I thought you were one of them," Brandon whispered.

Dixon shook his head. "Nah, these poor saps musta been part of another plan. There's probably five thousand prisoners in this hellhole. Ain't no way we're the only ones cooking up a plan. Speaking of cooking, were you able to get what I asked you?"

Brandon had made friends with a teenage girl named Jennifer, who worked in the kitchen. Once in a while she snuck him potato skins or food discarded from the guards' mess hall. This time she'd managed to smuggle out the bottom halves of some muffins left behind by a finicky guard at breakfast. Many of them hated American food and longed for the kinds of meals they were used to back home, but Naung-myon noodles weren't exactly easy to find in mid-America.

"It's back at the barracks," Brandon said, referring to the muffin bottoms, before Dixon slapped a hand over his mouth.

"Sometimes less is more, kid."

Brandon understood at once. Prison guards and

collaborators weren't their only concern. If someone overheard him divulge the location of contraband food, it wouldn't be there by the time they got back. When food was scarce, national and cultural alliances didn't mean a thing.

Dixon leaned forward and whispered, "And don't worry, our escape plan's coming along nicely. I'm gonna need you to keep an eye on a couple guard shifts and maybe gather some more food from Jennifer."

Reluctantly, Brandon nodded and then nudged his chin in the direction of the pug-faced guard standing over the last of the executed prisoners. "What's his name?"

"The one with a face only a mother could love?"

"Yeah, is he new?"

Dixon grinned. "His name's Lee Kun-Hee. Arrived last week and real eager to prove himself. I suggest you stay away from that one. He likes his job way too much."

"What about her?" Brandon asked, referring to a squat female guard who always seemed to be scowling.

"That little honey blossom is Yun Ji-Su. She kicked me in the ribs yesterday when we were planting soybeans in the eastern field."

"You weren't going fast enough?"

The smile on Dixon's face widened. "That's what she said. Work faster, work faster. But I think she likes me."

Brandon wanted to laugh but held it in. "If she bashes your skull in, you might need to start looking for a ring."

After the last of the dead were removed, Ellis delivered the commandant's final address. "Anyone foolish enough to think of trying to escape should know this—for everyone who escapes this camp, ten random prisoners will be put to death."

Brandon's guts clenched into a tight ball. It was one thing to risk your own life in a bid for freedom. If they failed they'd be tortured and executed. But if they succeeded, they'd be responsible for the deaths of dozens of innocent Americans.

Chapter 10

Back in Oneida, Diane and Emma stood on Alberta Street before the town's newspaper office, the *Independent Herald*. A two-story brick building that looked about as old as the town itself, the structure was scarred with the wounds of war. The upstairs windows had been broken by a squad of soldiers who'd used the second story as a firing position. The façade itself was dotted with pockmarks where bullets had torn away chunks of brick and concrete.

Although the newspaper had closed up shop right after the EMP, Diane and Emma were anxious to get inside to see if they could find anything that might help them print the thousands of propaganda leaflets they would need. A handful of old-timers had suggested they might find what they were looking for in the newspaper's basement.

Getting inside wouldn't be a problem. Soldiers preparing for the attacks had blown a hole in the wall to allow for rapid movement off the main streets.

Taking a final glance over her shoulder before she and Emma disappeared inside, Diane caught sight of a dense wall of cloud coming up from the south. The sight made her think of John and the dangerous mission he'd slipped away this morning to complete. They were well into the afternoon now and he still wasn't back.

To say she was worried was an understatement, but if she'd learned anything in these last few weeks, it was how to look strong when your very soul was racked with anxiety and pain. Gregory was still missing, along with Brandon. They'd gone off to the front in the thoughtless way so typical of teenagers with low impulse control. For reasons she couldn't understand, they'd felt this was the only way they could contribute to the war effort. But a long, dangerous voyage west hadn't been necessary since the war had found Oneida just fine on its own.

Diane had also learned that staying strong was just as important for the people around her. Creating a protective bubble to keep out the nagging concerns about her son's safety had helped a bit. Keeping busy helped more. If she was lucky, he hadn't been killed when the Chinese had smashed through the front lines protecting the Mississippi. The hope remained strong that he'd been sent to a POW camp and would wait there until a rescue could be mounted or they reached an end to this mad war. And that was why these leaflets were so important. Hope. The very thing which told her Gregory was alive and that she'd see him again soon.

Diane opened her flashlight and stepped inside, her mind shifting for a moment to the Colt .45 in the holster on her right thigh. They were safe, she reminded herself. Outside, hundreds of townspeople and soldiers were working feverishly to clear the streets. Spearing the darkness with her light, she caught sight of a room littered with papers and debris. Lazy dust motes floated through her field of vision.

"I think this door leads to the basement," Emma said.

Ever since her daughter had set herself the task of designing that leaflet, she'd started eating again—she had even put on some much-needed weight—which only strengthened Diane's conviction that idle hands were the devil's workshop.

"Let me go first," Diane said, waving the flashlight

beam.

The stairs creaked as they descended one step at a time.

Emma fell in behind her as they weaved past bundles of old newspapers, some dating back fifty years. They turned a corner and both saw it at once, a monster looming out of the shadows. A hand-cranked printing press. Stenciled on the side was 'SP-15 Vandercook' and below that 'Trademark 1965.'

"It's huge," Emma said. "We'll never get it upstairs."

She was right. In fact, it was a mystery how they'd even managed to get it down here in the first place.

Emma took hold of the crank and tried to move it without success. "Must be stuck."

Diane tried with the same result. "This beast's been sitting down here for decades, honey. A bit of oil should do the trick."

Two levels of shelving beneath the press contained ink, paper and tools for maintaining the machine.

Emma stepped around it to check the cylinder when she shrieked and stumbled back, slamming her shoulders against the wall with a boom. Startled, Diane rushed to her side.

"What is it?"

Emma raised a finger, pointing it at the Chinese soldier on the floor, his back against the side of the press. A dried pool of blood ringed his dead body. The front of his uniform had been pulled open to expose a gaping wound in his belly. She'd seen similar sights many times before in old Civil War photographs John had showed her of soldiers rifling through their own clothing searching for a wound. Back then, finding a gut shot was usually a death sentence.

"Don't worry, we'll get him out of here," Diane said, removing the .45 from her holster. They left in a hurry then for fear there might be others hiding in the building who weren't quite as dead.

Diane and Emma emerged to find Vice Mayor Ray Gruber pushing a wheelbarrow full of cinder blocks. He stopped, the smile plastered on his face fading. "You ladies all right?"

"We're fine," Diane told him, dusting herself off. She explained what they'd seen.

"I'm sorry you had to see that," he said, in the warm, gentlemanly way that often set Southern men apart. "I'll speak with General Brooks right away about having these buildings swept again."

Nodding, Diane couldn't help noticing Rodriguez looking down at them from the battered second story of the veterinarian hospital. He had a strange look on his face, as though he were taking mental notes, a sight which stood out in contrast to the bustle of manual labor going on around her. Who would be sneaking around taking notes? Suddenly, a warning light went off in her head followed by a string of red flashing letters. The name that it spelled made her scalp feel three sizes too small.

Phoenix.

"Diane?" Ray asked, reaching out to touch her arm. He glanced over his shoulder, without finding the source of her disturbance. "You don't look well."

She slid an arm around Emma, trying to shake off the nauseating fear that the traitor in their midst had found a way to leak the details of John's mission to the enemy. "Any word from John yet?" she asked.

Ray shook his head. "No, but spotters positioned on the water tower did see a flash in the sky, so my guess is they managed to get that A-bomb aloft after all."

No sooner had Ray finished his sentence than the air was filled with the sound of a prop plane engine. Diane's pulse began to quicken. The workers around them stopped and searched the sky, their hands propped over their eyes to block the late-afternoon sun.

Within minutes a Cessna swooped low over Oneida, dipping its wings to the roar of soldiers and citizens cheering their return. A group repairing the dentist's office broke into an impromptu rendition of *America The Beautiful.*

"O beautiful for spacious skies,
For amber waves of grain…"

Emma hesitated. "You think they all made it back?" There was a touch of desperation in her daughter's voice.

Diane couldn't help being caught up in the moment. "I'm sure they did, honey," she said. The jovial celebrations up and down Alberta Street were still going strong. All except for Rodriguez, who tucked away a notebook and disappeared.

Chapter 11

The conference room was far too warm and brimming with excitement. At one end of the table were John, Moss, Reese, Devon and Ray Gruber. On the other were General Brooks, Colonel Higgs and the rest of the general's military staff.

No sooner had Billy Ray set down at the Scott Municipal Airport than a Humvee had showed up, tasked with bringing them back to the mayor's office for a debriefing. Not surprisingly General Brooks wore the expression of a man who was about to eat his hat.

"First off," Brooks said, "we're glad you all made it back."

Reese's fingers went to his pocket before he clenched them into a fist.

"I'm sorry to say not all of us made it back," John told them. "Jerry Fowler was killed shortly after we released the balloon. We flew out of Oak Ridge right as the enemy was overrunning the place."

"An unfortunate, but necessary sacrifice," Higgs said with sincerity. The colonel was looking older than usual, in spite of his short-cropped silver hair.

"Without his background in meteorology," John added, "this operation would never have gotten off the ground. At some point down the road, when all this is behind us, it might be nice to erect a memorial for all the folks of Oneida who have laid down their lives."

"That would be nice," General Brooks said. "Although starting a monument might be a touch premature. Our first task is to win this war."

"When we arrived," John explained, ignoring Brooks' jab, "Colonel Porter's men were loading a steam train bound east with what looked like nuclear material and important documents. My hope is that they kept as much as they could out of enemy hands." John paused for a moment. "What about those Faraday cages? Did they hold up all right?"

"Most of them did," Higgs said. "A few weren't sealed properly and everything inside got fried. Some of the telephone and old power lines also began emitting a strange glow, but that couldn't have lasted more than a few seconds. All in all, I'd say we weathered that storm rather well."

"Thank God," John said. "When we're done here, I'll have Wilbur deliver a brief status report to General Dempsey via carrier pigeon. But we'll need to monitor things for the next few days to keep an eye out for any adverse effects caused by the EMP. We were only able to get it thirty miles into the atmosphere."

"I've already got a team in place doing just that," General Brooks told them. "There are a few items on the agenda we need to discuss first." He glanced down at a dozen sheets of handwritten notes strewn before him. "I've organized work groups tasked with clearing those streets. Anything salvageable, such as high-caliber weapons, will be removed and used to bolster the town's defenses. We've also collected a few hundred QBZ-03 assault rifles we can add to our weapons arsenal."

"General, if I may," John said, raising a hand. "I suggest you call off those teams you set to clear the streets and reassign them."

A deep frown formed across Brooks' brow. "Pardon me, Colonel?"

"Clearing away dead enemy soldiers and stripping vehicles is fine, but the rubble in the streets is a natural tank obstacle. Sure, we need to navigate through town, so perhaps some of the inner roadways can be cleared, but anything that stops a tank or an APC from breaching our inner perimeter is a good thing."

Brooks glanced at Higgs, who agreed.

But John didn't need to see that exchange to know he was right. Before leaving he'd felt an almost blinding compulsion to tell Brooks to stop making decisions unless he was consulted first, but needless to say that wouldn't have gone over very well. Sometimes in the military, as in life, rank trumped common sense.

Brooks let out a long sigh. "Fine. Was there anything else you wanted to add, John?"

John fought the smile tugging at his lips. "Yes, in fact there was. Has anyone gotten an update from Dr. Coffee on the cholera outbreak?"

This time Higgs responded. "Yes, the situation has stabilized. No new patients have been reported and the number of deaths has gone down."

"Good," John said. "What about Huan?"

"Our POW?" General Brooks asked. "What about her?"

"Well," John said, "I believe we've gotten everything we can out of her. Can she be used as a bargaining chip somehow? As it is, she's just another mouth we need to feed."

"And have her divulge everything she's seen?" Brooks spat. "Don't be foolish."

"Has she really seen all that much?" John wondered out loud. "I mean, we've kept her locked in a room since we captured her. I doubt there's all that much she could reveal. At least nothing more than those Chinese troops saw when we chased them out of town."

"If she's really served her purpose," Brooks said, "then maybe it's time we execute her."

The suggestion caused an immediate knot in John's

belly. Sure, she was the enemy. But killing for killing's sake was never a good policy. If anything, it only threatened the lives of their own citizens caught behind enemy lines or in some cases in North Korean concentration camps. A sickening image of Gregory and Brandon starving and pleading for help flashed before him.

"That'll only offer the Chinese a justification for even worse atrocities." John turned to Moss. "Any word on those leaflets Emma was working on?"

"I think she's only just started," Moss replied, leaning back in his chair. "My guess is if we put a few more people on it, we can have enough for a drop by tomorrow."

"What drop?" Brooks asked.

"Over the Jonesboro concentration camp," John said. "We need to let them know we haven't forgotten about them."

The expression on General Brooks' face made it clear offering hope to imprisoned Americans wasn't high on his list of priorities. "Anything else?" General Brooks asked, annoyed.

"The detonation of that EMP will surely cripple the enemy's ability to wage war. Now we wait for word from General Dempsey on what to do next."

"If he knows anything," Reese said, "he'll launch an attack as soon as possible."

"It would be wise if we leave the strategic decisions to those in charge," General Brooks snapped.

The look in Reese's eyes was calm, but John could tell the sniper was battling the urge to jump over the table and throttle the man.

"All right. This meeting is hereby adjourned."

They all rose from the table and filed from the room. All except for John and General Brooks, who was still gathering his papers. John went to him. "I think it's time we began getting Oneida on a war footing, don't you think? And I'm not only talking about soybeans. Once we get that power back on, as limited as it might be, we'll be able to create a small munitions factory and pump out mortars and Molotov cocktails."

As usual, Brooks looked skeptical. "Where are we going to get the metal and components for that kind of thing?"

"We have all the components we need."

"What are you talking about?"

"Mortar tubes can be made from schedule 80 steel pipe, the same stuff used as the electrical weatherhead on the houses in town. Another option is axle tubes from old trucks. Listen, everything we need is at our fingertips as long as we're open and creative enough to recognize it's there. All that's missing is power. And whatever we lack from wind, we can get from using engines from trucks and abandoned military vehicles. We've been on the defensive for so long we haven't had a chance to use what we've already got to get back on our feet."

"And what's to stop the Chinese from catching wind and bombing our factories into the ground?"

"Nothing," John said. "But my guess is right now they've got bigger fish to fry."

"Hey, if it'll get you off my back for a while, then go ahead."

John left and headed for the radio room, where he found Rodriguez reinstalling the equipment they'd kept sealed in the Faraday cages during the recent operation.

"I have a message for General Dempsey I need you to deliver to Wilbur."

"The pigeon man?" Rodriguez asked, plugging his earphones in.

John scribbled down the message on a small slip of paper: *Mission successful. EMP detonated with noticeable effect.*

Awaiting further orders. He folded it up and slid it into a tiny pouch Wilbur would later attach to the bird. "About that other thing we discussed earlier…"

"About suspects?"

John nodded.

"Nothing so far."

"Roger that. Keep looking."

John turned to leave the radio room only to find a female soldier standing in the doorway. She was a redhead in blue and black fatigues. The name tag on her chest read O'Brien.

"Colonel Mack," she said sheepishly.

"Yes. What can I do for you?"

"I believe I met your son at the front."

John's eyes grew wide. "Gregory?"

"He was with an older boy."

"Brandon."

"Yes, they were both very eager to fight." Her eyes fell. "I was there when the whole center line folded in on itself. It was pure chaos. We fled the front lines, but not before I saw that whole part of the trench surrender to the enemy. I hesitated to tell you before in case you were upset that they surrendered, but I figured, if it was me, I'd want to know the truth no matter what."

John swallowed hard, fighting back the tears. "So they're alive?"

O'Brien nodded.

He cupped her shoulder. "You did the right thing."

She smiled. "You're not disappointed in them?"

"Not in the least. They did the only thing they could. But it also means there's still a chance we can get them back."

Chapter 12

Knoxville, three hundred and sixty-five days before EMP

A month after returning from his final deployment in Iraq, John found himself at the Back Door Tavern on Kingston Pike, seated at the bar and working on his fifth beer. The mirror behind the bar showed a grizzled and tired man looking back at him. John's dark, normally neatly cropped hair hung past his ears, pulled back from his forehead with nothing more than the sweat of a man who hadn't washed in a handful of days.

The place wasn't so much seedy as it was small. Behind John was a row of booths and in the corner a pool table where two men cracked balls back and forth, a noise which made John jump whenever he heard it, although nowadays just about any loud noise set him on edge.

The tavern door opened, letting in his friend James Wright along with a burst of mid-afternoon sunlight. Lanky but powerful, Wright had served under John as First Sergeant while they were stationed at Camp Stryker in 2006, around the time that PFC Steven Hutchinson and PFC Ryan S. Davis had been abducted and murdered by insurgents.

While on deployment, the men in his regiment had taken to calling the sergeant Johnny Cash on account of his deep voice and obsession with striking it rich. Like so many other vets, Wright had also changed significantly since returning from Iraq. The most noticeable difference was that he hardly smiled anymore. James slid into the seat next to him.

Next to his empty beer mug, John's cell phone started to vibrate. Diane was calling him again.

"You gonna take that, LT?" James asked, watching the phone buzz away.

John glanced down at Diane's smiling picture on his display screen. "Not just yet. And stop calling me LT. It's John or nothing."

James nodded. "I can drink to that." He waved the bartender over, a fiftysomething in a tank top three sizes too small. "Two beers."

"I thought the wife told you not to come back here, that if she caught you drinking again she'd toss you out on your keister?" John asked.

"She did. Heck, I'm supposed to be at Jack in the Box, getting food for the fam. I'll just eat a mint on the way home and tell her the car ran outta gas." James' hand was on the bar, his fingers twitching. John pretended not to notice, especially since his often did the same.

The two drank in silence for a moment, but James wasn't able to sit still. His gaze kept returning to those two men playing pool, then to the entrance and back toward the emergency fire exit in the rear. John recognized immediately what he was doing. He'd done the same the minute he entered the bar. Wright was making a threat assessment and searching for possible routes of escape.

Over in Iraq, the risk of coming under attack had been a constant concern. It didn't matter if you were back at base or on a patrol. Death could be around every corner, behind a smiling face or a double-parked car. IEDs detonating under your vehicle, snipers shooting you in the throat, or insurgents lobbing mortar rounds into the base and running away—those were the forms that threat normally took. Never-ending danger and extreme frustration at an enemy who refused to fight toe to toe were just a few of the realities men like John and James had faced overseas, many of which they'd brought back with them into civilian life.

By comparison to a combat zone, the need for operational security in a tiny bar in Knoxville was slim to nonexistent, and yet the compulsion remained and, for John at least, was growing stronger every day.

John finished his beer just as his phone began to ring again.

"One more drink," he whispered to himself.

James was watching the phone as well, two men lost in completely different thoughts.

"I gotta go," James said suddenly. "You got this?" He was speaking about the tab. Like John, James still hadn't found a job.

"All good," John replied.

"I may be back later."

John laughed sardonically. "If I'm still here do me a favor and shoot me, will ya?"

James slapped him on the back, rolled off the stool and headed for the door. "Roger that, LT."

John bit his lip.

The tavern door peeled open, burning John's corneas again. When it swung closed, John found himself alone once more with his own dark thoughts and the sound of cracking billiard balls.

"You all right?" the bartender asked. She was blonde, or at least this month she was, her harsh features softened only slightly by too much makeup and the dim pools of light around the bar.

John glanced up. "Couldn't be better."

The bartender looked over at one of the pool players who'd sauntered over to order a drink.

"Two Budweisers, Viv," the man said, winking. He was smacking his lips on a wad of gum, made him look like a cow.

The bartender smiled. "Sure thing, Stan." She went to the fridge.

Stan leaned closer to John. He was somewhere in his forties, dark curly hair and a goatee. "I couldn't help catch that friend of yours called you LT."

"That's right," John answered, struggling to focus through the beer haze.

"You a Marine?"

John shook his head. "Army. 278th Armored Cavalry."

"Cavalry? I thought they got rid of horses and buggies a long time ago?"

John remained quiet.

"Cowboys and Indians, get it?"

"Yeah, I get it."

The smile on Stan's face wavered. "Hey, friend, loosen up, I'm just joking with you."

Staring down into his drink, John said, "See, friend, the problem is jokes are supposed to be funny. So forgive me if I'm not rolling on the floor busting a gut."

"Hey, if you can't take a joke, that isn't my problem."

"And it isn't mine if you can't tell one." John's voice was rising and now the pool player's friend was coming over. This guy Stan had been trying to antagonize him, had waited until Wright had left the place before having some fun with a guy who'd had too many beers. John's fist tightened around the handle of his beer mug.

"I'm not here for trouble," John told them. "Just back outta my space and we'll chalk it up to a misunderstanding."

"I'm not backing outta anything," Stan said. "You

vets think just because you fought in Iraq it gives you the right to cuss off anyone you like."

"I'm warning you."

"You're warning me?" Stan laughed. "Now there's a good joke."

He stepped closer and was in the process of raising his hand to jab a finger into John's chest when the beer mug shattered over his head. Stan's legs gave out at once and he flopped onto the floor. His friend looked on in horror, eyes wide, his lips parted.

In John's hand was what was left of the beer mug, the handle and a serrated edge which he held out in front of him.

"Get outta here before I call the cops," Vivian the bartender screamed.

John snatched his phone off the bar and staggered for the door, stepping over Stan's unconscious form in the process. The light outside was near blinding as he wobbled outside. His F-150 was out front and he went for the keys in his pocket before realizing his fingers were still laced through the remains of the shattered beer mug. He let it fall to the ground with a clink of breaking glass and noticed for the first time that his right hand was dripping blood. He wiped it on the leg of his black jeans and a thin gash appeared across his right palm.

In spite of the stinging pain and the shame he felt for what he had just done, John was also dimly aware that when he was drunk, he wasn't thinking about the past. He stumbled into his truck, started the engine and marshalled his powers of concentration to back up and work his way home.

He was driving down Kingston Pike when a call from Diane came in. John answered it.

"Where have you been? I've been trying to get a hold of you for more than an hour."

"I was interviewing for a job," John lied, adding to

the already horrible way he was feeling.

"Really? You never mentioned anything about that."

"I'll fill you in when I'm home. Did you need something from the grocery store?"

"No," Diane said. "I just got a call from Christopher Lewis' wife."

"My old JTAC?"

"Yeah, I've been trying to get a hold of you."

"I got that part already. What's wrong with Christopher? He in trouble?"

"No, John. He's dead."

"Dead? But how?" he asked, although part of him already knew the answer.

"He hanged himself."

John didn't say a word after that. The beer haze which had been hounding him since he got behind the wheel of his truck was suddenly gone. In fact, all John felt was a numbness, creeping up his legs and into his head. That was the only way he knew how to keep the pain at bay, to prevent it from taking over his soul, from destroying him.

Chapter 13

Oneida. Present.

The next morning, John awoke to find Henry in the radio room. All of the equipment was back in place and fully operational.

"Is there a message you need to get out, sir?" Henry asked, removing his headphones.

"It's four in the morning," John said. "Why are you up?"

Henry grinned. "I might ask you the same thing. The truth is, I don't usually get more than a few hours' shut-eye a night. I prefer to scan the airwaves, searching for other communities out there in all this mess. Many of them are isolated and afraid. Sometimes I'll find a family in a cabin somewhere behind enemy lines who've spent the last three days watching Chinese supply convoys heading east. After that latest EMP, it's been a good opportunity to get some data on damage assessment."

John couldn't help but be impressed. "There was something I'd been meaning to ask you."

"Sure thing."

"I can see how passionate you are about reaching through the airwaves to Americans on either side of the battle lines. Have you ever considered starting a radio program, one we would broadcast every day with updates from the front and tips on living off the grid?"

Henry practically beamed. He reached into a drawer and withdrew a sketchbook, flipping the pages until he arrived at a series of three-dimensional letters he'd drawn. Together they spelled *The Stand Against Tyranny*.

John stared down at it. "What's this?"

"My radio show. At least the one I'd been planning to start once the war was over."

"Why wait for the war to end? This is something we need now. Maybe even something we can use to help organize the resistance."

John was referring specifically to the Allied use of radio stations like the BBC during the Second World War. Members of the resistance would be given orders to hit specific targets or gather for larger operations by listening for key words spoken during an otherwise normal broadcast.

John started to leave and then planted his feet. "You know, my only problem is the name," he said.

"You don't like *The Stand Against Tyranny*?"

"It sounds too angry. You want something that'll motivate and inspire. How about *The Voice of Freedom*?"

•••

John was heading back to their living quarters when he saw Diane was awake.

"I can't say I'm surprised to see you up so early," she said, rubbing her tired eyes. "I came to find you after the debriefing with General Brooks and you were sprawled on the bed, passed out."

He smiled. "It was only supposed to be a quick nap."

"Maybe, but your body said otherwise." She went up and slipped her arms around him. "I'm glad to have you back in one piece."

His expression changed.

"I heard about Jerry," she said, holding him tighter.

"I wanna say he knew the risks, but he was practically shaking during the flight to Oak Ridge."

"He went out making a difference, John. Isn't that

what most folks dream of?"

"I still can't wrap my head around the timing of that Chinese attack."

Diane loosened her grip and stared into his eyes. "Ask any good detective and they'll tell you there's no such thing as coincidence."

"That's what's bothering me."

"Need I remind you your only proof Phoenix exists is the word of a single POW who was being tortured?"

John frowned. "Not when she mentioned the spy she wasn't. I could understand if we were in the middle of waterboarding her and she threw it out there to get us to stop, but that confession happened long after."

Wringing her hands behind his back, Diane let go and pulled away. "I've been going back and forth about something, but after what you just said, I feel there's something I should tell you."

"You're not pregnant, are you?"

"Oh, stop. Of course I'm not. It's about Phoenix."

John grew more serious as Diane told him how she'd seen Rodriguez acting suspiciously yesterday.

"I appreciate you saying that, Diane, but I'm pretty sure Rodriguez is clean."

"Are you sure, John? I mean, how can you be?"

"Well, I can't be certain about anyone but myself, can I?"

She looked hurt by that and he reached out to her, but she moved away from his outstretched hand.

"Look, you know what I'm trying to say. No one's beyond suspicion. I'm sure there are people wondering about both of us. It's just after what Huan said about a spy in Oneida, I couldn't help looking at the cholera outbreak with a different set of eyes. Right now, I've got people trying to figure out who Phoenix might be. They've drawn up a shortlist of suspects and each of them is being looked into, and if you must know,

Rodriguez is one of the people doing the sniffing."

That seemed to satisfy her, although John had learned long ago that once Diane got an idea in her head, it was hard to break it loose.

"At this moment, Diane, the town needs your help getting back on its feet. Getting the greenhouse back up and running. Canning what food we have already. And I was thinking that some of the street lights might be used in the greenhouse once the power is restored. Ray Gruber and his boys are trying to fix the damage the windmills sustained during the battle. We need to find creative solutions to problems that didn't exist before the EMP."

He'd been trying to tell her to back off playing sleuth as nicely as he could, but it didn't matter how well he sugarcoated it, Diane knew exactly what he was saying.

"There's something else I think you should know," he added.

"I'm not sure I want to," she replied, moving to the kitchen where she began fiddling with a sink full of dishes.

"I guarantee you will. A young private stopped me yesterday after the debriefing to say she remembers seeing Brandon and Gregory at the front."

Diane stopped what she was doing.

"She said she saw their position being overrun."

"Oh, no, John. I don't want to hear it. Not if you're gonna give me bad news."

He went and gently pulled her hands away from her ears. "She saw them surrendering to the Chinese. Which means they may still be alive."

All the air came out of Diane's lungs at once and she fell limp into John's arms. "Oh, thank God." She was quiet for a moment, probably saying a prayer. "So let's go get them."

"It's not that easy. We need to wait and see if

General Dempsey's planning a counterattack. In the meantime, we need to get those leaflets out. How soon can Emma have them ready?"

"Tomorrow," Diane replied without hesitation. "I'll go over there myself and start cranking them out."

A sharp knock came at the door. John opened it to find Henry, a crease of tension along his forehead.

"What is it now?" he asked, dreading the answer.

"It's Huan, sir."

"Our POW? What about her?"

"She's gone."

Chapter 14

The beam from their flashlights bobbed up and down as John, Henry and three soldiers rushed to Huan's holding cell. Oneida was on lockdown, the major avenues in and out of town guarded by small units tasked with keeping an eye out for Chinese incursions. If Huan's training was anything like what American pilots received in SERE—survival, evasion, resistance and escape—then she'd know better than to travel via a major roadway.

Up ahead were the cells. A steel door secured that part of the jail from the rest of the building and a guard was posted outside twenty-four hours a day. The door to the cellblock stood ajar, but more disturbing was the body lying on its back, hands clasped over its throat. Dried blood stained the soldier's fingers, his eyes locked in an expression of shock and horror.

"It's Cooper," Henry said. The man on the floor had been on guard duty. "We've sent teams with tracking dogs to run her down. With any luck, we'll have her back within the hour."

I doubt it, John thought as he bent down on one knee. The soldier's throat had been slashed with a sharp knife. The line across his neck was almost surgical. "Box cutter?" John asked.

Henry flashed his light to gain a better look, his face registering discomfort. "Or a scalpel."

Dr. Coffee's face flashed in his mind's eye. "Go to

the doctor's house and bring him in for questioning," John instructed one of the soldiers, who nodded and ran off.

John stepped carefully over Cooper's body and into the holding cell area. One of the cell doors was open in an otherwise empty room. On the floor was a set of keys.

"So the killer approaches the guard," John speculated, "maybe engages him in small talk or distracts him somehow and then slashes his throat."

"Why not just shoot him?" Henry asked.

"No way. Too loud. This had to be quiet to give Huan enough time to escape." John paced back and forth. "If this was a citizen looking for some payback against the Chinese, then we would have found Huan's body hacked to pieces."

A vivid memory of Rwanda came to him. After the genocide, the streets were filled with survivors of brutal machete attacks. In most cases, their bodies still bore the disfiguring signs of attempted murder. It was the kind of sight you never got used to.

"This was someone from town," John said. "An inside job."

Henry seemed puzzled. "Really? How can you be sure the Chinese didn't send some super-assassin?"

"Two reasons. The first is that a special forces operative would likely have used a silenced pistol rather than risk hand-to-hand combat. I mean, look at this hallway, they would never have gotten close enough before Cooper drew on them. Second, Cooper's pistol was still in his holster and take a good look at the expression on his face. He knew this person and a knife across the throat was the last thing he'd expected."

For some reason, John hadn't wanted to believe Phoenix existed, let alone that he or she was behind this, but so far everything he'd seen pointed in that direction.

It was still early dawn when they left the crime scene, but already the town was in full swing. Soldiers and citizens were moving house to house in search of Huan. If they could recapture the Chinese pilot they might be able to learn Phoenix's true identity. John was still busy overseeing the search when Rodriguez found him.

"They need you back at headquarters," he said.

"Have they found her?"

"No, but General Dempsey's on the radio and he wants to speak with the senior leadership."

•••

The radio room was packed by the time John arrived. General Brooks and Colonel Higgs were already there along with Moss and Ray Gruber. They'd started without him.

"Congratulations again on a fine operation," General Dempsey said. "We're getting reports the Chinese support infrastructure's been crippled for nearly a two-thousand-square-mile radius."

"It was touch and go for a while," General Brooks said, taking the glory without batting an eyelash. "But we managed to pull it off."

Moss glanced over at John and shook his head with disgust. It seemed Brooks' sneaky move to take credit for the EMP mission was even beneath him.

Truth be told, John didn't care. The important part was limiting the enemy's ability to wage war and he had done that. If Brooks was positioning himself to tack another star on his helmet, that wasn't going to lose John any sleep. He had his time in Iraq for that.

"The Chinese are well dug in right now along our front lines," Dempsey said. "We've estimated their strength at close to a million men. American reinforcements and stockpiles of fuel are moving up every day from the east, but just not fast enough. Not to mention what's left of our air assets, which we're keeping grounded until we can deploy them to full effect."

"General, does that mean you're postponing the attack?" John asked from the back.

"That you, Colonel Mack?"

"It is, sir."

"I won't feel comfortable committing our boys until we outnumber them by at least two to one."

John closed his eyes in disbelief. "Sir, are you not worried that this might be our only opportunity to strike the Chinese when they're so vulnerable?"

"I am, but I think you're overstepping a little, Colonel." Dempsey sounded defensive. He probably wasn't accustomed to entertaining alternative points of view.

"I tend to agree with the general on this," Brooks said, predictably. "If our attack should fail, then we risk losing what little we have left."

"And if we do nothing, then the Chinese will eventually find the men they need to push through whether we like it or not."

"I won't commit," Dempsey told them, "unless I know their supply lines are virtually incapable of moving men and materiel to the front."

John was beginning to worry they had another General McClelland on their hands. It was said that if the famous Civil War general outnumbered the enemy three to one, he'd swear he couldn't attack unless he had ten-to-one odds.

What the Americans needed was a commander from the Ulysses S. Grant school of warfare. Someone who wasn't afraid of sending men into battle, who could push the enemy back on his heels and then once he broke pursue him until he was destroyed. That was the strategy that had worn down the Confederacy and helped win the

Civil War.

It didn't matter that that war happened over a hundred and fifty years ago. Technology might have changed, but by and large, people didn't. A Union soldier's terror as he stared down the gleaming barrels of Confederate rifles on the fields of Antietam was the same fear American GIs faced coming under fire in the jungles of Vietnam.

The meeting went on for another few minutes, but John had largely tuned it out. General Dempsey's mind was made up and nothing would change that. Not surprisingly, there was no mention of Huan's escape or their suspicions that Phoenix was behind it. John suspected that General Brooks was covering himself. Seemed these top brass guys spent far too much time playing politics and too little time playing general. He wanted to remind the man that positioning oneself for high-ranking office wouldn't mean much if they lost the war.

After they were done and everyone left, General Brooks paused briefly on his way out.

"Next time, Colonel Mack, I suggest you show a little more respect for your senior commanders. You may think you're a big shot after that EMP stunt, but anyone can be demoted."

"I'm not interested in rank," John replied. "I just want my country back."

Brooks walked away without responding. At last the room was empty when Moss came back in.

"I think it's time for a haircut," John said, in a vain attempt at humor.

"I'll consider it," Moss replied. "Listen, some of these guys couldn't fight their way out of a paper bag."

"Maybe," John said. "But they're the ones in charge,

not us. I'm afraid our hands are tied."

"Are they?" Moss replied, one eyebrow cocked.

"What are you getting at?"

"The general said himself he wouldn't budge until he was sure the Chinese supply lines were broken."

John scratched his chin. "You're talking guerrilla warfare."

"I'm saying hit them where they least expect it." Moss was growing more excited. The veins in his neck were bulging.

"But we don't have enough fuel for any kind of armored convoy," John said before his eyes lit up. "But we do have something else. How many horses we have at the stables?"

"Don't know. A dozen, maybe more."

"That's how we'll move around," John said, working out the logistical requirements.

"Like Jeb Stuart," Moss shouted. "I'm gonna need to find me an old cavalry hat."

A Confederate cavalry commander during the Civil War, Jeb Stuart had been known for his daring raids around Union lines, capturing supplies and harassing Union troops.

John shook his head. "Unfortunately, we may have to aim somewhere closer to Bloody Bill Anderson."

"The guy Jesse James fought with during the war?"

"Yes, and it sickens me to even think of acting in such a way, but those PLA soldiers need to fear us worse than death itself. With any luck, we might be able to reach out to other pockets of resistance. Many of them lack any sort of direction. If we can help motivate and transform them from being a nuisance into a nightmare, we can stop the Chinese dead in their tracks."

Rodriguez appeared just then.

"What now?" John asked. "Tell me you have some good news for once."

Smiling, Rodriguez said, "Some soldiers from the 3rd Infantry Division have just showed up. They said they were routed down near Oak Ridge and won't be able to make it back to friendly territory. A bunch of them talk about Oneida like it's some sort of oasis."

"I suppose it is," John said. "Moss, you'll need to set them up at the high-school barracks with the other soldiers and check with Diane to make sure our food supplies are okay."

"Will do."

Rodriguez went to leave and then spun around. "Oh, nearly forgot. That first batch of leaflets are done. Billy Ray and some redhead soldier named O'Brien are flying out shortly to drop them over the Jonesboro concentration camp."

The news was good indeed and John smiled. Not simply with the hope that Gregory and Brandon might see they hadn't been forgotten. But for another reason. An idea had just occurred to him. One that might devastate the Chinese supply lines and give General Dempsey exactly what he was looking for.

Chapter 15

The five-gallon pails of water were growing heavier in Brandon's hands with every step. When he wasn't in the fields planting seeds or tilling soil, he'd been ordered to bring water to the prisoners who worked in the camp kitchens. It was a sweet job, a step up from the other most sought-after occupation in the camp: bathroom attendant. Before the EMP and the invasion, any work that involved cleaning a row of open-pit toilets would have been considered inhumane. No question, the stench was hard to bear, but the payoff was hard to beat. Four walls and relative privacy from sadistic guards. The North Koreans rarely went near the place on account of the overwhelming reek and so whoever was charged with sweeping and keeping the building clean could also save themselves from a beating or two.

Brandon's part-time job bringing water to the kitchen staff put him in a unique position. If he was careful, he could trade information or items he scavenged around camp for food. Most often that meant whatever ended up as trash, but once in a while—the muffin bottoms being a prime example—he managed to score something he didn't need to scrub the dirt off of. This time he'd brought a small travel toothbrush he'd traded for a handful of apple skins.

Brandon arrived at the kitchen's back entrance. A dark brown wooden structure, it still smelled of fresh paint, another indication of how new this nightmare really was. He knocked and after a small wait, the cook,

Sammy Stevens, answered the door. Dressed in a dirty white uniform, Sammy wore a small white hat and sported a thick New Jersey accent.

Over Sammy's shoulder, Brandon spotted two guards inside the kitchen, chatting to one another. This was another cushy job, maybe the cushiest, and for the guards as well since they would constantly pick at the food under the guise of taste-testing.

"Is Jennifer here?" Brandon asked, handing over the first bucket of water. Weevils coated the surface, but the prisoners had learned quickly enough to skim them off with the tips of their fingers.

Sammy pulled his hat off his head, revealing a short-cropped and greying head of hair. "You didn't hear?"

"Hear what?"

Sammy looked around to ensure they weren't being overheard. The two guards near the kitchen line were still busy chatting. "That group that got executed the other day. She was one of them."

The weight of the terrible news hit Brandon like a body blow. For a moment he wasn't able to speak.

"I know," Sammy said, reading Brandon's shock. "We all felt the same way. She musta got caught up with the wrong crowd. I mean, who's dumb enough to think you can escape from this place?"

Brandon nodded absently, the numbness creeping down his neck, into his chest and his legs.

A prisoner crossed the doorway behind Sammy, looking like a ghost. Brandon's eyes followed him, compelling Sammy to look as well.

"Oh, that's Brice. He's been here about a month. Just got back from a stint in the re-education program."

"Brainwashing?"

Sammy snorted discreetly. "At the very least, my friend. Most of the poor schmucks who make it back look like they ain't got no one home. Some wise guys joke he's haunting the place, but it ain't too far from the truth." Sammy glanced over his shoulder and then took the second bucket of water. "You didn't bring anything with you today, did you?"

Brandon felt for the toothbrush he'd put in his waistband and pulled part of it out so Sammy could see. He was still reeling from the news that Jennifer had been killed. She'd been one of the few new friends he'd made in camp. She couldn't have been older than sixteen or seventeen.

"Toothbrush, eh? Well, those fools behind me are supposed to be doing an inspection, so I got nothing to give you right now, except some information."

"What about?" Brandon asked. In here, information was power and could be purchased along with just about anything else.

"News from the front. A town called Oneida."

Brandon's ears perked up. "Really? I'm from there."

Sammy smiled, pulling his cap forward. "Toothbrush first."

Sighing, Brandon handed it over. "I wanna hear everything."

"Well, I'll tell you what I know, let's start with that. Way I heard it, when he was on the outside, one of the new guys used to listen to the radio. That was before a Chinese patrol caught him hiding in the basement of some house and sent him over here. Anyway, he told me that after the Chinese army busted through the Mississippi, they pushed all the way to the Appalachians. All except for two places. A junction east of Knoxville and this tiny, one-street nothing town in northern Tennessee called Oneida."

Brandon's jaw slackened as his mouth fell open.

"That's right, they kept attacking the place until dead Chinese soldiers were stacked on the streets like cord wood. Can you imagine?" Sammy's voice rose for a moment in jubilation before he caught himself, checking behind him to be sure the guards hadn't overheard. After that, the smile on his face returned. He bent down on one knee, skimming the weevils off the top of the water. "They're calling your home town the new Bastogne."

Now Brandon was also smiling, but his newfound joy was simultaneously fraught with concern over whether anyone he knew had been hurt or killed. His mother and sister, John… Emma.

Brandon left after that, a whole slew of emotions swirling around. He passed by the front gate to observe who was on duty and see if he could find out how long they'd been there for.

By now he knew all the guards' names and a little something about them. Even North Koreans, cruel as they could be, sometimes couldn't help divulging little bits and pieces. Information that could come in handy as he, Dixon and others laid the foundations for their escape.

Marching outside along the fence line were two male guards: Lee Kun-Hee, who Brandon called Pug Face, and a thin older man named Shin Chang-Jae. Lee's tendency for cruelty was well known, but Brandon had learned that Shin had a weakness for white women and often stood glaring at the girls in camp as they went to and from the fields. The rumor floated around that Shin was even responsible for some of the pregnancies Brandon and the others had seen. Vile as it was, these were the sorts of details Dixon had ordered him to gather and so he had, as faithfully as possible.

With his discreet observations complete, Brandon was preparing to head back to the barracks when the sound of a plane caught his ear. He planted his feet for a moment, watching as the noise became louder and louder. This wasn't a jet, nor was it a helicopter. It sounded like a single-engine Cessna and it was coming straight for them.

A number of the guards had also heard it and were scanning the skies, but they were searching too high. Whoever was flying this thing was coming in low. Then he spotted the plane as it cleared a clump of trees in the distance and closed on the camp. Those around him stood transfixed at it approached, all probably wondering the same thing. Were they about to be bombed or was this poor guy lost?

Now the prison guards had their AKs poised and ready to fire, but as the plane came within a hundred yards they all saw the colors of the Chinese air force painted on its wings and body. This was one of theirs, which made its strange behavior even more puzzling. Thirty yards from the gate, it pulled up and flew directly over the camp. The door on the side of the plane opened up as someone began pushing what looked like blocks of paper out through the narrow opening. The blocks of paper broke into thousands of tiny pieces, each of them fluttering to the ground. The Cessna flew the length of the rectangular prison camp, releasing its payload, before tipping its wings and veering off.

All present, guards included, were left scratching their heads at the strange spectacle. But the answer to their question was fast approaching as hundreds of papers seesawed to the ground around them. It was snowing and Brandon hadn't seen anything so beautiful in a long time. He stooped down and picked one of them up.

There he found a pamphlet with the picture of a giant fist pushing aside a column of Chinese tanks. *Stay Strong*, it read. *Victory is Close at Hand.*

He'd seen this style before in the scrapbook Emma was often doodling in, but it was only when he flipped the paper over that the air was nearly sucked from his lungs.

To B.A.,
Don't lose faith.
Love, Emma

Brandon scooped up a handful of other papers and saw the same message on each. B.A. could only be him, Brandon Appleby, and Emma was the girl he missed so deeply it hurt.

That was when the guards began shouting at anyone they saw collecting the propaganda leaflets. Shots rang out and two prisoners who were bent on one knee collapsed to the ground. Brandon stuffed as many as he could under his shirt and raced back to the barracks. If he knew the guards, they'd begin by searching every bunk and prisoner for leaflets as soon as possible. There wasn't a chance he was going to let them tear the hope from his hands and his heart. He would dig a hole and bury them.

The message from Emma seemed clear enough and Brandon struggled to contain his elation. John and the others were coming to free them. He wasn't sure when, but they were coming, and when they did, Brandon would be ready.

Chapter 16

Following the EMP, the law offices of Stanley & Walton in Oneida had been used as both a storehouse for dried goods and, later, a firing position for an M60 machine-gun nest. Currently, it was serving as the secret headquarters for the special operations team John was putting together.

Not surprisingly, Stanley and Walton had been among the first to flee the town following the initial strike, but although they hadn't been gifted with bravery, they had had the foresight to situate their offices far enough from the main strip—Alberta Street—allowing John to keep its new purpose safe from prying eyes.

The group was slowly assembling in Sam Walton's old office. Pictures of the rotund man in a variety of daring pursuits still littered the walls. Arapaima fishing along the Amazon, hang-gliding in the Alps. By the looks of it, the man had an appetite for adventure. What a shame he'd tucked tail and run away so early. Especially since the chances were good he'd ended up in a North Korean camp somewhere.

Soon, most of Walton's things would be removed and the room transformed into a proper headquarters. For now, the large map of the Eastern and Central United States was all that betrayed its true purpose.

Already waiting in the spacious room were Moss, Devon and Reese along with a half-dozen soldiers handpicked from various units for their expertise in unconventional warfare. When all twenty-five men were accounted for, John began.

"I'm sure each of you is wondering why you're here. As you have probably heard by now, the EMP we detonated over Oak Ridge has severely disrupted China's ability to ship men and materiel to the front. We've even gotten word that Russian forces are also running into major problems. Although their supply lines are greatly diminished, they need to be destroyed. From the group assembled here, fifteen of you will make the final cut."

The men looked from one to another.

"Each of you has been chosen because of a unique skill or ability you bring to the table. Some of you have a proficiency with explosives, others marksmanship. Many of you have served in Iraq, conducting raids and counter-insurgency operations. As you'll soon see, even this will serve us well. The only thing I don't have from you yet is your consent. I've invited each of you here to make you an offer, to become a member of a team tasked with going behind enemy lines to kill and disrupt the enemy in any way we can."

The room was quiet for a moment, although several of the men were smiling.

"Who can say no to that?" a soldier from the 3rd Infantry Division named Taylor asked.

John shook his head. "You'd be surprised. But coming along isn't an order, it's important you men understand that. In fact, your commanding officers don't even know we're having this meeting." He paused while some of them shifted in their seats. Others looked on without moving a muscle. "The need for operational secrecy here doesn't mean we're doing anything illegal." A handful showed disappointment. "But if you make the final cut and you consent to joining us, then I'll speak with your commanders about releasing you. There is one prerequisite that isn't negotiable. Candidates must be able to ride."

Taylor put his hand up. "You talking horses, sir?"

John nodded.

The soldier's grin spread. "Where do I sign?"

But not everyone felt the same way and John could read it on some of their faces. The consent element was important for operations like these. It wasn't simply about issuing orders and hoping your authority was enough to push your men along. There was a good chance what they faced out in the field would push them far beyond their comfort zone. He needed men who were daring and willing to risk their lives, but he also needed soldiers who knew when a tactical withdrawal was the best course of action. In other words, he needed people who demonstrated the very creative thinking the enemy lacked.

A brawny soldier in the front row raised his hand. "When do these selection trials begin?"

Special forces groups like the SEALs often put applicants through gruelling trials designed to weed out the weak. It was better, they argued, that such cracks were spotted early, rather than on a mission when the lives of fellow soldiers were on the line.

"They began the minute you walked in that door," John told them. "Now, if you don't mind, I'll have you all move to the office next door. If any of you wish to bow out, now is the time to do so."

"I've never ridden a horse," a sergeant with the 101st said. "But that doesn't mean I don't want to join you, Colonel."

"There's no need to explain." John turned to the rest of the men before him. "None of you will be judged for saying no. There's no shame in it."

And with that they stood and moved to the other room.

Only Moss, Reese and Devon stayed back. "What do

you think?" Reese asked.

"You know all their names?" John asked. "And the faces that go with them?"

Reese waved a list of names he'd written on a paper. "Sure do. You might be surprised to learn that most snipers that I've met were horrible remembering faces. Throw a picture of the target they'd killed into a photo lineup and they'd never be able to ID 'em in a million years."

"Really? Why is that?" John asked.

"Hard to say. My guess is it's easier to shoot a man if you can pretend he isn't a human being. You know, like shooting at paper targets. Might be one of the reasons the faces on those things are blanked out. Goes against a man's innate programming."

"What does, killing?"

Reese laughed. "Nah, accepting the fact that you killed a person and not a monster."

John took the list from Reese. "I already know who I want."

"Really?" Moss said from the other side of the room.

"Anyone who flinched when I mentioned that their commanding officers didn't know about this, they're the ones I crossed off first. We need men who obey orders, but not someone who's scared to make a decision on their own." John scratched off a handful of other names. "Next anyone who seemed uncomfortable when I mentioned the horses." He ran a line through a few more names. "And finally, anyone whose face didn't glow at the notion of killing Chinese soldiers."

"I didn't think we were looking for bloodthirsty killers, Colonel," Devon said.

"Homicidal maniacs, no. Someone who won't hesitate to pull a trigger, yes." Even speaking the words, John couldn't help thinking of his own issues with taking a life. It was never something to be relished. Probably every major religion in the world condemned killing and yet it was an inescapable reality on the battlefield. The him-or-me mentality one experienced while firing a machine gun at attacking troops was one thing. It was either kill or be killed. But when there was a choice involved, that was another beast altogether. One that still haunted John's dreams.

Chapter 17

Once the selection process had been completed, John had been left with fifteen men, including Moss, Devon and Reese. John himself would be number sixteen. While the selection process had been painless, his conversation with General Brooks asking for their temporary release had been far more difficult. Brooks had wanted to be briefed on the mission they were about to undertake and John had deflected his attempts with all the grace of a punch-drunk boxer. In the end, only a reluctant promise that the general would be fed into the loop as soon as they returned made Brooks finally relent.

With that behind them, the newly formed special forces unit met once again at their new headquarters.

"We'll be heading out in two teams," John explained. A table had been brought in and the map from the wall laid over it. "The first team will be only four men—Taylor, Phillips, Jackson and Campbell. Two of you have explosives training, the rest are on fire support. Your mission will be to lay IEDs along the stretch of Interstate 40 between Nashville and Knoxville. According to our sources, it's become one of the main Chinese arteries for supplies coming from the west."

Heller, another explosives expert, looked uncomfortable. "So you want us to become glorified Iraqi insurgents? We were fighting those guys overseas."

"Every bullet and grenade, every loaf of bread and

ball bearing that reaches the front represents more American soldiers killed."

"I get that, sir," Heller replied. "I'm just saying it feels weird to be on the other side of things now, is all. I wish we could hit them head-on like we've always done before."

"You're right," John admitted. "America's talent has usually been to charge our enemies head-on and tear them apart if they ever dared to stand up to us. But that wasn't always the case. Have you ever heard of the Minutemen?"

Heller suddenly didn't look so sure of himself. "I think so. Didn't they fight during the Revolution?"

"That's right. They were sharpshooters from Kentucky, known for their long rifled muskets and the deadly accuracy with which they used them. Their specialty was picking off British officers in order to sow fear and confusion amongst the Redcoats. I'm sure it won't come as a surprise to hear the British hated this tactic—they called it ungentlemanly conduct on the battlefield. Maybe the Kentuckians wondered themselves if they were breaking some sacred code. But guess what, it worked, and if I need to adopt the tactics and strategies of our enemies in Iraq to save our country, then I'll do it without batting an eye."

Heller grew quiet.

"We're about to become guerrillas, folks. And not the hairy kind." John looked at Moss, anticipating some lame joke that never came. "I know that's what you were thinking, don't lie. *Guerrilla* is Spanish for 'little war', a term coined for the small bands of men who stood up to resist Napoleon's invasion of Spain. But this isn't about the past, gentlemen. This is about the future. The four of you will set off as soon as this meeting is done, work your way on horseback down to I-40 and destroy as many convoys as you can."

Another hand went up. Specialist Santos. "But won't the Chinese start to redirect troops to protect the roads and stop us?"

"We pray they do. Every unit pulled off the front lines brings us a little closer to our objective." John turned back to the map. "The rest of us, twelve altogether, will make our way to Paragould, Arkansas. With most of their transport trucks useless, the Chinese have been conducting a desperate search for older vehicles. Our mission will be to hit that depot and destroy as many of those vehicles as we can."

Reese was leaning over John's shoulder when his finger plopped near a map marker indicating the depot. "That's less than ten miles from the Jonesboro concentration camp," he said, surprised.

John's eyes glazed over for a moment with the thought of his boys and the suffering they were surely experiencing. "I know it is," he replied, choking down the agony that was bound to come from being so close and yet so terribly far.

Chapter 18

"If you're putting yourself in harm's way," Diane told John as she closed the notebook before her, "it's better you don't tell me anymore."

They were back at their residence. John had come by to tell her he was leaving for a little bit.

"I think you're right," he agreed. "These days we can't be too careful." He glanced down at her notebook. "How are the greenhouse repairs coming along?"

She nodded. "Fine."

"Tell Ray I expect those windmills to be up and running by the time we get back."

"I'll pass the message along, but you know what he's gonna say."

"'Those Chinese really banged us up good.' Yeah, he'll make a joke out of it, the way he makes a joke out of everything. Just pass the message along and I'll deal with it when I get back."

John hugged her and turned to leave. He stopped, certain Diane was about to say something.

"I'm making a list of suspects," she finally admitted.

John pursed his lips, still staring down the hallway. "You know how I feel about that."

"You're only trying to protect me, I know," Diane said. "But I may have an idea on how to catch Phoenix."

"Just promise me you won't do anything rash. Remember what happed with The Chairman. You nearly got yourself killed."

She agreed and John hoped she wasn't simply telling

him what he wanted to hear.

He left the mayor's office and made his way to the town newspaper. Inside on the main floor were a man and two teenaged girls. Each of them was using giant paper guillotines to cut out leaflets. The drop over Jonesboro concentration camp had been a huge success and they were already planning drops on other camps behind enemy lines. The teenagers pointed John downstairs, where he found Emma, a thin layer of perspiration on her brow and arms as she cranked the printing press lever.

"That's tough work," he commented with surprise.

His presence startled her and she gasped. Her expression shifted when she saw he was wearing his tactical gear.

"Don't ask," he told her. "Your mother and I have already been over it."

"Once I'm done with this batch, we're going to need some more paper," she said.

John nodded. "Speak with Ray. He'll get you what you need. You've been working hard, Emma. Maybe it's time you take a break."

She grabbed the lever and began cranking it. "When I'm done here, I gotta go home and feed George." She was referring to the goose he and Brandon had captured over by Stanley Lake. The cantankerous little guy had survived the battle huddled next to Emma down in the sewers. Since then George had been working up quite an appetite. "I owe it to Brandon until he gets back," she said.

John found himself in the middle of one of those dreaded moments every parent went through—the moment where you could either give your child a dose of reality, in this case that Brandon might never be coming home, or you could smile and tell them what a great job they were doing. After all, every bead of Emma's sweat was a testament to her dedication to fanning the flames of other people's hope. Who was he to snuff that out?

"Is that where you're going?" Emma asked, taking her hands off the lever and putting them on her hips. "To bring the boys home." She grew still and held her breath.

"I can't say right now, honey. I hope you understand that. Remember how I used to tell you about the last world war and how the British had that expression, 'Loose lips sink ships.' I don't want to get your hopes up, but I also don't wanna sink any ships. You understand, I hope."

"Yup," she replied with obvious disappointment and went right back to work.

Feeling her pain, he leaned in, kissed her forehead and headed for the rendezvous point.

Chapter 19

He arrived at the stables a few moments later and found the horses already saddled and loaded with gear. The four soldiers on the IED team were off to one side going over tips on wiring and planting bombs. Their brash young leader, Taylor, was talking about his time in Iraq and how insurgents began by digging holes in the ground to plant IEDs before graduating to hiding explosives in donkey carts and road kill.

Nearby the eleven men who would accompany him on the raid to destroy the Chinese truck depot were assembled. Moss stood before them, going over the plan.

John called them together for a last few words. As they closed in, Taylor raised his hand.

"What is it?" John asked.

"I noticed the horses the IED team is taking are loaded with wooden planks and shovels. I'm just wondering if we're gonna be digging tunnels like the Viet Cong?"

This elicited laughter from some of the men.

Humor aside, the idea had occurred to John, but the sheer immensity of the country made the use of tunnels impractical. Only weeks before, the Chinese forces had been holed up on the crest of the Mississippi river. Today their front lines were stretched along the Appalachian mountain chain. In the coming days or weeks it was impossible to tell where they'd be. Would they be washing their feet in the Atlantic or retreating in haste toward the Rockies?

John let Moss take the floor to explain how the IED team was to begin creating camouflaged weapons caches at key locations. Whatever ammunition and weapons they captured on their raids would be deposited inside these storage areas. He made sure they understood they weren't simply digging a hole and throwing guns and ammo inside. The ammunition needed to be protected from the elements and kept within certain temperatures.

"Once you've dug the hole," Moss told them, "fill the bottom with a layer of gravel or rocks, then about fifteen inches of sand. This will help drain any water away that seeps into the cache. On top of the sand place logs and then the wooden floorboards which will hold the ammo crates. Keep them spaced apart to allow air circulation. For the roof, you can use leftover boards or several branches. Pile leaves over that and dig a drainage ditch around the cache to collect runoff. If you can find some PVC pipe and endcaps that are large enough, you can even store a limited amount of ammunition in there."

"I've also had Devon make each team some of these," John said, holding up a small, sharpened triangle.

"Caltrops," Taylor exclaimed, unable to hide his exuberance.

"That's right. They're also pretty simple to make, using three-inch nails, filing off the end, bending them at a ninety-degree angle and then welding them together. They can be tossed across a roadway to puncture tires during an ambush or used to create a slow leak. Be creative, but above all, don't hesitate to use the tools we've given you if the situation gets sticky. And remember, the most successful missions are ones where the enemy never knows you were there."

"Until the place goes kablooey, that is," Moss said, his hands forming an explosion.

John stood. "All right, time to mount up, gentlemen.

And follow the paths through the Chinese lines we've outlined."

"Hold on," Taylor squawked. "We can't just ride off, not without a name."

Moss, Reese and Devon turned to John.

"He's got a point," Reese said, flipping out a cigarette and clamping the filter between his front teeth. "You got anything off the top of your head, Colonel?"

John drew a blank. Finding a name for their unit hadn't been high on his priority list, but he could see how important it was to the men.

An image of Teddy Roosevelt flashed before him. Not many people knew the twenty-sixth president had led a cavalry regiment during the Spanish-American War. They'd been called the Rough Riders and to John, given they were about to spend the next few days in the saddle, the name seemed strangely appropriate.

The men cheered upon hearing it and laughed at the reasoning behind John's suggestion. And with that they split into two groups, none of them entirely sure how many would ever make it back.

Chapter 20

John's immediate team was quiet as they cut through the dense forest trails on their way past the ring of Chinese troops encircling Oneida. Calling it a ring wasn't entirely accurate. The enemy had choked off every roadway into town. Creating an actual ring of soldiers would have required a deployment of thousands. It was the American armor they were really trying to keep in check.

Whenever possible open fields were to be avoided. Cover was their friend and a map of the Cumberland trail which passed through the wooded areas close to their objective was as invaluable as the weapons they carried. Before long, these maps would no longer be needed. These back trails in and out of Oneida would be seared into his men's memories.

Two days into their journey, they hadn't seen much activity. The roads, whenever they came into view, were largely empty save for the rare military convoys. It wasn't the hustle and bustle John had expected. In a way, it reminded him of how some fellow soldiers had described Afghanistan. The land was spread out and you could go for days sometimes without seeing either friend or foe.

In the evenings they made camp, avoiding a fire whenever they could. Many of the men ate MREs or canned tuna. Water from streams as well as carrots and hay kept the horses fed and happy.

It wasn't until the third day, when John's backside had gone from sore to numb, that they came upon a strange sight. Through a loose screen of trees, they spotted the edges of a neighboring town. Stretching up past the roofs of the buildings was a church steeple.

"You see what I'm seeing?" Reese asked, pulling up beside him.

John lifted the binoculars and adjusted the focus. "Looks like a church to me," he replied.

"Look where the cross used to be."

It had been knocked off.

"It isn't the first time I noticed it either," Reese told him. "I know those Chinese aren't big fans of worship. What little they do tolerate is usually so mixed with Communist politics, a bunch of the Catholic groups in their own country have gone underground. I suspect the same is starting to happen here."

"As painful as it is to see," John said, "we need to pick our battles."

So far, crossing the Mississippi had been the most dangerous part of the operation. The concern of being spotted had meant using the old Caruthersville railroad bridge near Dyersburg.

It was later that day that they arrived at their objective. Set on the outskirts of Paragould, Arkansas, the truck depot was huge and situated next to a rail line. It appeared the Chinese were shipping in a mishmash of vehicles via older steam locomotives. John guessed there were well over a hundred trucks within the fenced enclosure. A handful of guards on foot stalked the perimeter. They were so far behind enemy lines, if anything went wrong, it would be a long and dangerous trek home.

Camped along the edge of the St. Francis wildlife reserve, they split into four groups of three men.

Seconds later, teams one to three crossed the open field and used bolt cutters to enter the perimeter fence. Group four remained behind with the horses and equipment. If the operation fell apart, each team would head back to Oneida on its own predetermined path. This way they couldn't all be scooped up at once.

John was with team one, which consisted of Moss and Devon. Reese would stay behind as part of group four and provide the infiltrating units with sniper cover and overwatch. Upon reaching the fence line, John raised his index and second finger in a v shape to call forward the soldier with the bolt cutters. The others waited, weapons at the ready, pulling rear and flank security. Within seconds they were through the chain link, the cut fence pushed back into place to avoid rousing suspicions. They weaved between the parked trucks. A combination of landmines and phosphorous grenades attached to rudimentary timers would do most of the damage.

John gave the signal and the three teams broke in different directions. They might not have explosives for all of the vehicles, but the hope was that vehicle fires would spread and take out as much as eighty to ninety percent of what was here.

Ten minutes later, with all the explosives in place, they returned to the fence. John scanned the treeline and spotted the all-clear signal from Reese. One by one they shuffled out and moved in teams back to the rendezvous point.

John's team was last to leave the area. He checked his watch. Ten minutes to go until detonation. One more pass by the perimeter guards and Reese waved them forward.

"Everyone accounted for?" John asked, after he,

Moss and Devon caught up with the others.

Reese nodded. “Yes, sir. Should we saddle up?”

“Not yet,” John replied.

“Are you sure?” Moss said. “Don’t we wanna be as far away as possible when those bombs go off?”

“Our position is safe from flying shrapnel, if that’s what you’re worried about. But I wanna see how long it takes the reinforcements to show up. At the first sign of them, we’ll pull back into the woods.”

They waited for a few more minutes when Reese spotted a convoy of military trucks approach the depot.

“Hey, we’ve got company. Three soft-tops. Can’t tell yet if they got any troops on board.”

“Heck, we may just kill two birds with one stone,” Moss said, rubbing his hands together excitedly.

“All right, those soft-tops have pulled up in front of the gates and are unloading…” Reese’s voice trailed off.

“What is it?” John asked, raising his binoculars and getting an answer he hadn’t expected.

The men being led off the soft-tops weren’t Chinese or North Korean soldiers.

They were American civilians.

Chapter 21

"What do you make of it?" Reese asked.

"I'm not sure," John replied. "Going by the expressions on their faces and the way they're being forced to line up, I'm not entirely sure they're willing participants."

"Truck drivers conscripted by the Chinese?"

John nodded. "Looks that way." These men were innocent civilians and they were about to be blasted into smithereens. A squad-sized group of Chinese soldiers were with them.

Tension rising up his neck, John checked his watch. "We got less than a minute." What was he to do? Let them die, sacrificed like the countless other civilians throughout this ugly war?

"There's nothing to be done," Moss said. "Wrong place at the wrong time, man. That's all there is to it."

"I got the Chinese squad leader in my sights," Reese said, staring through the scope. "He's got sergeant's stripes."

John bit his lip.

"What you want me to do?"

"Take him out," John shouted.

Reese glanced over at him. "Before the detonation? You sure?"

"Yes, do it."

Glancing back through his scope, Reese made a single click left on the elevation knob. Then he released a long slow breath as his finger settled over the trigger and squeezed. He'd brought the suppressed Remington 700 this time and it kicked back into his shoulder, making a dull clank as the round was ejected at nearly four thousand feet per second.

John watched through his binoculars as the shot hit the Chinese sergeant in the neck, spraying blood on the American civilians standing in loose formation before him. The Chinese soldiers around ducked for cover, shouting orders and scanning around fearfully. In the chaos the Americans broke free and ran. Ten seconds later the first landmine detonated, destroying a group of closely packed U-Haul trucks. On the heels of that came a second explosion, then a third and soon the entire depot erupted in a gout of twisted metal and flames. The heat was so intense, even from here John could feel it warm his cheeks.

The rest of the men mounted up while John and Reese remained concealed on the ground, waiting to observe the enemy response time. John's watch ticked away the minutes. At last, two ZBD-08s appeared and stopped near the rows of burning trucks. Then a handful of soldiers on motorcycles sped past them and down the road.

"How long was that?" Reese asked.

John checked his watch. "Nearly twenty minutes."

"Not great."

"It is for us."

Both men slid away from the treeline and headed for their horses.

"We homeward bound, boss?" Moss asked.

"Not yet," John replied. "We have one more stop to make."

John felt the tension among his men spike. He might not have come right out and said it, but they knew perfectly well where that next destination would be.

The Jonesboro concentration camp.

Chapter 22

As John and his Rough Riders were making their way south toward Jonesboro, Brandon was dropping seeds into small holes dug by a prisoner five feet in front of him. Scanning his surroundings, he saw thousands of American POWs draped in the same vomit-brown uniforms. Those who'd been here from the beginning were often reduced to skeletons in tattered clothing.

Brandon wondered when the North Koreans would replace the scraps some folks were wearing, especially since winter was marching steadily closer. He wanted to believe that even the heartless North Koreans had enough sense to preserve the very workforce which helped to feed them, although as the days passed, he'd begun to understand their disregard for human life. First the re-education program, then the breeding program and now the never-ending executions only served to reinforce the idea that this wasn't about the war effort or forging ahead with a twisted North Korean version of America. This was about slow and painful extermination.

Brandon also understood those sorts of feelings needed to be controlled. For now, his mind was all he had left, the only refuge where he could pretend he was once again in Oneida with Emma and the people closest to him. The note he'd seen on the leaflet told him he hadn't been forgotten. They knew he was still alive and right now that was worth more than a mountain of table scraps.

He'd met with Dixon a handful of times over the last few days, mostly in the bathrooms where the guards wouldn't bother them. Dixon refused to divulge any part of the escape plan other than to say that it was coming together nicely. Brandon had told him about the message on the leaflet and how help was on its way, but Dixon didn't buy it. There was no way he was going to sit and wait for help that might never arrive.

The man had a point, but what alternative did they have? If they managed to break out, they would be forced to live with the knowledge that their actions had led to the retribution killings promised by the camp commandant. Nothing in Brandon's life had prepared him to make that kind of decision. But one thing he knew for certain—after that leaflet drop, Gregory's resolve had started to waver. Upon hearing that Oneida had stood strong in the face of the Chinese assault and that a rescue attempt might be in the making, Gregory had predictably opted out of the escape plan. It seemed his fear of being shot in the back crawling under razor-wire fences was greater than his reluctance to be left behind.

The thought of Gregory made Brandon scan the field, searching for the boy. He spotted him about a hundred meters away, churning soil with his hands. Brandon was about to turn away when Pug Face shouted at Gregory and, when he didn't respond, knocked him to the ground and began kicking him.

•••

Barely ten miles away, John recognized the camp's close proximity provided too good an opportunity to pass up. Trails inside the St. Francis State Wildlife Reserve led from Paragould south toward Jonesboro and would provide the cover they needed to stay out of sight.

Once they arrived, their unit would remain concealed inside the woods. This portion of their mission would be devoted entirely to reconnaissance. The attack on the truck depot, important as it was, had only been a dress rehearsal, a test to see if his men could work together under stressful conditions.

The lightning bolt of inspiration which had hit John the other day had had to do with the camps. With the very real possibility that Brandon and Gregory were alive and being held captive inside, John had a burning interest in helping them escape. But committing Oneida's meagre resources toward such an obviously self-serving goal was irresponsible, verging on criminal.

It was during his conversation with Moss that the perfect solution had come to him, one he'd kept secret even from Diane. It called for his team of guerrillas to assault the Jonesboro camp, converting the people inside from prisoners into an armed resistance movement. Some of the earliest civilian prisoners were in rough shape, but the hundreds and maybe even thousands of military POWs hadn't been there for more than a few weeks. On their own, in hundreds of small groups, they could melt into the countryside and establish bases from which to launch their own attacks on other camps. John envisioned a long line of dominos, tumbling one after another as their numbers grew. With their ranks swelling, so too would their ability to tighten the noose on the disastrously overstretched Chinese supply lines. By then, General Dempsey should have the clear advantage he wanted. At least, he'd be hard pressed to find a reason not to attack.

Lying prone beside a maple tree, John peered out through his binoculars. The camp itself was rectangular, surrounded by a twenty-foot-high razor-wire fence—probably not electrified, especially now. Guard towers were spaced apart at hundred-yard intervals. It wasn't long before he spotted prisoners in rags working the fields, tilling soil and planting seeds.

"Something tells me this food isn't for them," John told Moss on his left. "Keep an eye on the guards—where they patrol, whether they're alone or in pairs, what they're armed with. How many extra magazines they're carrying."

Most prison guards rarely expected to fire their weapons, let alone engage in a sustained firefight. Not when they could use the butt to bash in a disobedient prisoner's skull. That meant when the time came to assault the place, the guards on the ground would quickly run dry on ammo. The ones in the towers, however, were likely better supplied. But that was where men with Reese's expertise came in handy.

"I've got movement near the front gate," Reese said, watching through his 10x scope.

The activity was frantic with vehicles coming and going. More likely than not, it had something to do with the mission John's men had just pulled off.

In the field, it looked like there was a commotion going on. A group of guards approached a small prisoner—a child around Gregory's height and weight—and began beating him.

"You seeing what I'm seeing?" Reese asked.

"I am," John replied, his heart beating in his chest. Not only at the way his fellow countrymen were being treated. The boy who'd stood up to that guard looked an awful lot like Brandon. As if that wasn't torture enough, John knew there was nothing he could do about it without jeopardizing the greater mission. Any hope of freeing the camps might mean watching his loved ones executed before his very eyes.

Chapter 23

Gregory looked up, frightened and in pain, trying to dodge the kicks and punches. Pug Face slammed the toe of his boot into the side of Gregory's head, making his body go limp.

Brandon shouted and began running toward them. From off to his side, other guards screamed in Korean. The crack of AKs being fired came next, kicking up a patch of dirt at Brandon's feet. That was when Pug Face unslung his rifle and pointed it at Brandon. His heart pounding with fear and rage, Brandon raised his hands, searching Gregory's prone form for signs of movement. Two of Ellis' American deputies showed up and dragged the boy away. Gregory's eyes fluttered as they whisked him away.

Pug Face shouted something guttural Brandon couldn't understand. He flicked the end of his rifle into the air, a move Brandon understood to mean, 'Get back to work.' The urge to charge the ugly little guard was nearly overpowering, but even in his rage, Brandon knew the move would be fruitless. John had taught him many things in the previous months but dodging bullets wasn't one of them. Reluctantly, he turned his back and returned to what he'd been doing, aware that at any moment he might be shot in the back for daring to stand up.

As Pug Face settled down and moved on, one thing had become perfectly clear. Regardless of the consequences, Brandon and Gregory needed to leave this place or it was sure to become their final resting place.

•••

Later, after roll call, Brandon made his way back to the barracks. He'd hoped to get word on Gregory and whether he was doing any better. A kick to the head could mean concussion or, with little to no medical care, something far worse. He arrived to find Ellis and his deputies tearing the loose woolen blankets off each bunk and checking underneath the thin foam mattresses which covered them. Prisoners crowded the doorway, frightened.

"What's going on?" Brandon asked.

An emaciated man next to him whose prison garb looked about as weathered as the man himself raised a bony finger. "They caught wind of another escape plan and now the whole camp's going nuts. I heard Sheriff Ellis has spies he uses to sniff out the escapees. Looks to me like they hit pay dirt. I just hope the commandant doesn't start bayoneting the rest of us."

"He isn't a sheriff," Brandon said. "Not anymore. He's a traitor and the worst kind."

The man shrugged. "Maybe so, but I'd be willing to bet he's convinced himself he's saving lives."

Brandon sighed, watching them tear the place to shreds. This wasn't the first plot they'd uncovered. In fact, it seemed every other day a handful of so-called escapees were being rounded up and bayoneted. "Any word on who they caught?"

"Nothing certain, but I did see 'em haul off a mouthy soldier named Nixon…"

"You mean Dixon?"

"Yup, that's him, and they had a boy with them too.

Had to be carried away since his legs were real wobbly."

Skeletal fingers danced up Brandon's spine. He didn't need to be given any more details to know who the skinny man in the tattered uniform was talking about. They were accusing Gregory of being part of the escape plot and now he and Dixon would both be executed.

•••

Brandon tore around to the back of the barracks, searching for the patch of earth underneath the wooden building's framework where he'd hidden the leaflets. He dug through the dirt with fingers already raw from his work out in the fields. Finally he spotted a patch of white, grabbed the top leaflet and filled the hole back in. His next stop was the camp kitchen where he knocked several times. Finally, Sammy answered, looking concerned.

"Water run?"

"No, I need you to do me a favor."

Sammy didn't look so sure.

"Remember how you told me about those people who sneak up to the fence line, leaving food and tradeables?"

"Yeah."

"Do you think they'd be able to deliver a note to Oneida for me?"

"That's kinda far, don't you think? On the off chance their radio's still working, maybe they could send the message that way."

"Give me a pen."

"Geez, kid, you're killing me here." Sammy plucked a pen from behind his ear and handed it over.

Brandon scribbled a few words on the leaflet and

then handed the paper to Sammy. "Keep this well hidden till you can get it into the courier's hands."

When he turned to leave, Sammy called after him.

"Hey, my pen."

Brandon stopped and handed it over.

"Now where are you off to in such a hurry?" Sammy asked, folding the message and tucking it under the band of his pants.

Brandon drew in a deep, nervous breath. "To speak with the camp commandant."

Chapter 24

What John had seen from outside the fence line of the North Korean concentration camp near Jonesboro had weighed heavily on him during the entire trek home. They had made the journey in record time. Seeing Brandon and his son in mortal danger had created a sense of urgency within him. But more than that, seeing the conditions at the camp—Americans dressed in rags, used as slave labor, beaten and probably killed at the slightest provocation—had made the need to free the camps so much more pressing.

They returned to Oneida to puzzled looks. No one knew about their mission and he'd told his men to keep it to themselves, at least until he gave the all-clear. Sure, some details were certain to slip out in the days to come. But Phoenix was still on the loose, and word of their plan leaking out might cost the lives of many Americans, including their own.

Once the horses were cleaned and back in their stables, John, Moss and Reese climbed into a four-seater golf cart and headed onto Alberta Street. Their next destination was the mayor's office, where they hoped to find General Brooks. They didn't get more than a few hundred feet, however, before John slammed on the brakes. Visible over the tops of the buildings were the spinning blades of both windmills. John turned the wheel hard and headed for the football field and the greenhouse, both of which sat in the windmill's shadow.

They arrived to find a small crowd gathered around what appeared to be a glowing light bulb. Many watched it with utter amazement. A pine shack nearby was also new.

When Diane and Emma saw them approach, they peeled away from the others. Emma threw herself into John's arms. Diane waited her turn with a warm smile, her head tilted slightly in the late-afternoon sun.

"Do I need to check you for wounds?" Diane asked.

"You won't find any," John told her. "At least none that are visible."

"So what do you think, Dad?" Emma asked him. She was giddy for the first time in a long while.

John shook his head. "I didn't think it would ever happen."

Ray Gruber came over, brimming with grins and no doubt a ton of bad jokes.

"I gotta say, I'm proud of you Ray," John told him. "They're both beautiful."

Ray laughed. "Until the Chinese come and knock them down, right? I've also set up a series of lawnmower generators in the new shed I built. Each is connected to an alternator, which charges a battery bank. They're real noisy, but will serve in a pinch if anything should happen to my creation."

In Ray's mind, he'd conceived and built the whole thing himself. It didn't seem to matter that dozens of others had also helped make it a reality. Every man had his foibles, John supposed, a failure of the flesh even he wasn't immune to. "I didn't know mower generators were even possible."

"Adapting them wasn't all that hard, but we did have trouble finding a pulley that would work. Finally settled on a two-and-a-half-inch pulley. Just took some trial and error, was all."

John and the others excused themselves and headed

back to the golf cart. Diane followed after them.

"Did you at least succeed in whatever mission you went on this time?"

John slid into the driver's seat. "We did. But every success only reminds me how much we have left to do."

"One step at a time, John. You start getting ahead of yourself and mistakes will happen."

"You're right, honey, but unfortunately this next step can't wait."

Chapter 25

Knoxville, three hundred and fifty days before EMP

The days following the news of Christopher Lewis' death had been particularly hard on John. The warm summer temperatures, the lush foliage along the streets in Sequoia Hills, even the sound of children playing outside, none of it seemed to make things any better for him. Not the way it used to when he was in a rut.

Over the last week, John had also taken to sleeping in his truck. He'd begun to feel as though the rooms in their house were too large and unsafe for him. And before long, he no longer felt safe or secure unless he was in a small, cramped space. Even so, sleeping was something of a misnomer, since John hadn't gotten a proper night of it since he returned from Iraq. This was his most dreaded time of day. If he was lucky, a dozen beers or a bottle of Jack Daniels would slide him into a dreamless stupor.

Diane hadn't understood much of what he'd been going through, but she'd respected his wishes. The VA (Veterans Affairs) had told her John would require time to reintegrate back into civilian life and she was trying to be as understanding as possible. Soon enough, however, John's need for his own space had meant that he'd sometimes pull into the driveway and not enter the house at all. Getting a serious buzz on had been the only way to keep those thorny memories at bay.

Sometimes, when he did manage to get some shuteye, he would wake up shouting orders to ghostly mortar teams to check their fire. The weight of being responsible for another man's life was a heavy one indeed. He'd read an article years ago about a scientist trying to find the weight of the human soul. The scientist had conducted a series of experiments and eventually arrived at a measurement: twenty-one grams. Thinking back to how many men he'd lost in combat and post-deployment suicides—and the crippling strain of those lost souls pressing down on his shoulders every day—John knew that number couldn't possibly be right. It had to be more. Much more.

Pulling into his driveway after a night of hard drinking, John spotted his neighbor Al Thomson, sitting on his front porch, enjoying the warm weather. John killed the engine and reclined his seat, ready to sleep off another evening of too many beers.

He hadn't been more than a few minutes into his oblivion when a rap came at the window. At once, his hand went for the S&W M&P .40 Pro he kept under the seat before he realized who it was. John gave the key a quarter turn and lowered the window.

"Fine night, isn't it?" Al asked, peeking inside the truck.

John looked around, the cab spinning around him. "If you say so."

"Everything all right, John?"

"Sure," he replied, vaguely aware of his slur.

"You didn't have a fight with the missus, did you? We have a guest bedroom in the basement if you need somewhere to sleep."

John tried to smile. "Thanks, Al, but I prefer it in here. I tend to keep Diane up at night, so I've gotten in the habit of making alternate arrangements." He tapped the steering wheel, as if to say, *She might not look like much, but to me she's home.*

"How'd you get that cut on your hand, John?"

"Oh, this? It's nothing, I was just taking out the trash."

Al stared at the wound, straining to see in the dim light cast by the truck's overhead lights. "I'm no doctor, but I think that could be infected. You might wanna have it looked at."

John glared at the cut, having trouble focusing. "Nah, I think I'm fine."

"You didn't drive like this, did you?"

"What's with all the questions, Al?" John barked. "I'm just trying to get some sleep here."

Just then a light came on in the house and Diane appeared.

"Oh, great, now you've gone and woken up my wife."

Al watched Diane as she approached.

"Why don't you come inside, honey?" she asked John.

"I don't wanna disturb you or the kids."

"Well, believe it or not, you're disturbing them every time you sleep out here."

John was suddenly terribly embarrassed she was speaking so frankly in front of Al.

"There's a cut on his hand that I'm worried about," Al said.

"I thought you were going to get that treated," Diane said.

"I will. Tomorrow."

Al pulled a hanky out of his pocket and wrapped it around John's hand. Now Al's wife Missy came over. This was turning into a crowd, making John more and more uncomfortable.

"Why don't you come inside," Diane offered. "I'll set up the pull-out couch for you."

Without being prompted, Al opened the door and helped John out of the truck. He landed on a pair of wobbly legs, grabbing onto his neighbors' shoulders for support.

They headed inside and brought John to the sofa in the living room. Gregory and Emma stood in the kitchen, watching all this unfold.

"Thank you," Diane said to Al and Missy.

"Don't mention it," he replied, ruffling Gregory's hair. "Who knows, maybe one day we'll be the ones in need of a hand. That's what neighbors are for, isn't it?"

After they left, Diane sent the kids to their rooms so she and John could talk.

"James Wright called the house," Diane told him, opening a wicker trunk where they kept extra blankets and pillows. "Said you weren't at Christopher Lewis' funeral. You know, I told you I was happy to go with you."

John shook his head. How was he supposed to explain that being there was too difficult?

"The drinking's starting to become a real problem, John. Susan Wright and I have started talking on a regular basis now. Commiserating, you might say. James has been hitting the bottle and it's gotten to a point where she's about to throw him out. Is that where you want things to go with us?"

John shook his head, patting the plush pillow.

"I think you should go and talk to someone at the VA."

"You mean a shrink?" John spat with disgust.

"I'm sure it'll help."

"And then what, Diane? Have them label me a coward?"

Tears came to her eyes. "Ever since I've known you, John, you've always been under such control. I've never seen you like this."

"I can handle it."

"No, you can't. That's exactly the problem. You always take too much on yourself and fail to do the most important thing."

"Really? And what's that?"

"Ask for help. No one's gonna brand you a coward, John. If not for yourself, do it for the kids. Think of your JTAC friend Christopher Lewis. You don't want them growing up without a father, do you?"

On a bookshelf beside the television was a row of framed family pictures. A handful were of Gregory and Emma learning to water-ski two summers ago, beaming with joy and pride at what they'd accomplished. But more than that, John knew part of the joy the kids had experienced came from knowing their parents had been watching them grow.

The thought made John's body convulse as tears fought past his closed eyelids and rolled down his cheeks. The floodgate he'd tried to keep closed for so long had burst right off the hinges.

Chapter 26

Oneida. Present.

John, Moss and Reese found General Brooks inside the high-school gymnasium. Ever since shattered elements of the 278th, 101st and now the 3rd Infantry Division had trudged back into Oneida from the front, the secondary school had become something of a barracks. Classrooms on the top floor were now sleeping quarters for officers. The rest housed enlisted men and support staff. Although many of the kids in town were probably dreading the day lessons would resume, John couldn't wait. It would signal a return to normalcy, a feeling he hadn't known for quite some time.

When he arrived, the energy in the gymnasium was frenetic. On his way he'd spotted small groups of soldiers running through town, leaving him wondering if everything was all right.

Brooks gave two soldiers a list of names and asked for them to be brought in for questioning.

"What's going on?" John asked.

Brooks stopped, resting a hand on a crate of ammunition. "Two women fetching water from the reservoir this morning found Wilbur Powel dead, along with all of his pigeons."

John gasped. "I thought we'd assigned a guard to him."

"We had," General Brooks said, pushing past John, Reese and Moss. He scooped up a clipboard from a table behind them. "But after Huan's escape, we needed every available man to run a house-to-house search."

"Did you find anything?"

Brooks shook his head. "We even brought Dr. Coffee and his son in for questioning, but their alibis both checked out."

Moss crossed his arms. "Guess you didn't think World War Three would have you playing detective, did you?"

"Speaking of detective," Brooks said. "Where were you three between 0200 and 0600 hours?"

Reese smiled. "We'd tell you, General, but then we'd have to kill you."

"We were conducting reconnaissance," John answered, deflecting Reese's well intentioned, but ill-timed joke.

"Reconnaissance?"

"Yes, it's the reason we've come to talk with you. In fact, you'll need to get General Dempsey on the radio. I know the Chinese are still struggling with their electronics, but I'd feel more comfortable if we used an encrypted signal."

"Can it wait? I'm in the middle of something here."

"I'm sorry, sir," John said. "But it's urgent. Perhaps Colonel Higgs could take over for you."

Brooks sighed and let his clipboard fall back on the desk with a clatter. "You're the most stubborn subordinate I've ever met. I just want you to know that."

John's chin dimpled with a grin. "Now I know you and my wife have at least one thing in common."

•••

"All right, John," General Dempsey said. "You've got the secure signal you wanted, now let's make this quick."

"Understood, sir. My team and I just got back from destroying a truck depot near Jonesboro, Arkansas. I've also got another group planting IEDs along I-40 to destroy Chinese supply columns heading east. But the real reason I'm on the line with you, sir, is about the concentration camp right outside Jonesboro."

John spent the next few minutes outlining his plan for liberating the camp and arming the freed prisoners.

"What sort of state are these men in?" General Dempsey asked. "Will they be in any condition to mount guerrilla raids if you succeed in breaking them out?"

"I won't lie, General. The folks we saw were dressed in rags. In the short time we were there we saw at least one prisoner beaten and dragged away. Many are American soldiers who were deployed along the Mississippi when the Chinese overran our defences. That means they haven't been there more than a few weeks. But the longer we wait on this, the worse they'll get. The last thing we want is to be marching sick and weakened POWs hundreds of miles to safety. By launching the raid now, we might just be able to start a chain reaction. The Chinese are overstretched. Without a doubt, conquering a country as vast as ours presents a unique set of challenges. I'm sure a conversation with Napoleon and Hitler about pushing into Russia would show you what I mean."

"I'm very familiar with both campaigns, thank you. What do you need from us then?"

"I've already got a dozen men," John replied. "And all I need is an extra fifty. Much of that will depend on how many more horses we can get our hands on."

"What about dirt bikes?" Moss threw out. "I'm sure we'd be able to find at least a dozen of those around town."

"We'll also need to speak with David Newbury," Reese added. "He showed up from the Jonesboro camp a couple days before the Chinese attacked. Was on his way south to see his family, I believe."

"He still here?" John asked.

Moss shrugged. "Heck, he could be halfway across the state for all I know."

"We'll go look for him," John told them. "He may be able to provide us with a ton of useful intel."

"All right then, Colonel," General Dempsey said. "Good luck and Godspeed."

After that, Henry chopped at empty air with his hand to indicate the signal had been dropped.

General Brooks came next to John.

"I've doubted you before, Colonel, and each time you've proven me wrong."

"I get no pleasure in it, General. Things don't always turn out the way I'd planned."

Brooks nodded. "Do they ever?"

Another wave came from Henry as he pressed the headphones against his ears.

"Maybe it's General Dempsey," Moss said, "changing his mind about the mission."

Reese laughed, searching himself for a cancer stick.

But the troubled look on Henry's face told a different story. "Is there anything else?" he asked whoever was on the other end before pulling off his headphones and swiveling around. "I just received a message from Brandon, leaked out of the Jonesboro concentration camp."

John's chest suddenly constricted.

"Well, come out with it," Moss said.

Henry's eyes found John and John knew his day was about to get a whole lot worse. "Gregory's been accused of trying to escape. He's been slated for execution."

That image of his son, crumpled to the ground and

then carted away, was playing back in John's mind on an endless loop. He could have risked the lives of his men and charged in there to rescue the boys, could have done something to stop what was happening, but that would have been the reckless act of a selfish leader. As a commander he had passed a difficult test. As a father, he had failed miserably.

If nothing else, the message from Brandon had made the situation perfectly clear. They didn't have weeks or even days to prepare and rehearse for an attack on the camp. They had hours—and the seconds had already begun ticking away.

Chapter 27

The following two hours were spent putting together the rest of the assault force. John opted to fill it with soldiers from what remained of the 101st. Many of them had been in the thick of battle during the Chinese attack on the town and he wanted men who had fought together. Contrary to popular perceptions, combat was just as much about knowing the man next to you as it was about proficiency with your weapon. The same was also true in professional sports. Even an all-star team could fall flat if the players didn't gel.

John had sent Moss and a handful of other men south toward Huntsville in order to get as many more horses as they could. He would wait until they returned before revealing his plan.

With the troops taken care of, John switched his attention to gathering some last-minute intel. Devon entered the Rough Riders headquarters then, blond and baby-faced.

"Did you find—" John stopped when he saw the thin man trailing behind Devon. He had disheveled black hair and was skinny as a rake. John wondered if he was well enough to do this.

"I was down with cholera for a while," David Newbury said. "So in a sick kind of way, you folks are lucky. If I had my health I woulda been long gone." He seemed to notice the sudden concern in everyone's expression. "No need to worry, I got a clean bill of health from Dr. Coffee. All's I gotta do now is start putting some weight back on before I head south and find my family."

"We won't keep you long," John told him. "We simply have a few questions about the camp you were being held at near Jonesboro."

The muscles in David's face tensed. "I was hoping you weren't gonna ask me about that. I saw a lot of good people die in the short time I was there."

"A month, as I understand it," John said.

David nodded. "Maybe, but I'll tell you, it sure felt like a lot longer than that."

John motioned for David to sit. He did the same and began tapping his index finger on the desk. "You remember how many guards were at the prison?"

Leaning back in his chair, David exhaled loudly. "Gosh, I haven't a clue. Somewhere between one and two hundred, I suppose. Far fewer than the number of prisoners, that's for sure. Always struck me as strange how such a small number of guards could control thousands of inmates."

"They mess with your head," Reese said, standing near the doorway. The imposing Barrett M82 was at his side, as though he expected John to give the order to move out at any moment. Either that or he couldn't wait to get going.

"This is true," David agreed. "But they also have another way. Those North Koreans find you guilty of a crime, doesn't matter how minor, they don't just lock you away, they imprison everyone in your family. And I'm not just talking brothers and sisters, mothers and fathers. I remember meeting fifth cousins in the camps doing hard labor for relatives they didn't even know existed. It's insane."

John's finger-tapping sped up. He was trying to stay

focused and not let the emotional part of him get swept away. "You mentioned you were let out to forage," John said.

"Yeah, one group of prisoners was tasked with preparing the soil nearby for cultivation and another was sent with guards to forage the area for anything edible. This was how they were feeding us at first. I can't say whether that practice is still going on."

"Back to those guards. Can you remember how they were armed?"

"Sure can. They never hesitated to stick the barrel of a machine gun in my face or shove the butt into my guts."

"Did they have extra magazines on them?"

David paused. "Don't think so. No handguns either." He smiled weakly. "You can probably tell I don't know a lot about guns. Point and shoot, right?" He molded his index finger and thumb into the shape of a pistol.

"No, you've been a great help so far," John said. "What about the soldiers' barracks and officers' quarters?" John laid down a rough sketch of the camp as he remembered it. "Do you remember where they're located?"

David pointed. "The guards' barracks and officers' quarters are all in the center of camp around a central courtyard. That's where they execute people." The muscles in David's emaciated face grew slack. "You folks aren't thinking of attacking that camp, are you?"

John shook his head. "No, just collecting some information." He paused for a moment. "Why do you ask?"

"I've seen how those North Koreans operate. If you're going you gotta get everyone out. And don't leave anyone behind because they'll surely be killed, along with all of their relatives."

Chapter 28

Once they were done with David Newbury's debriefing, John and his lieutenants moved to the planning room where Colonel Higgs awaited them. They found the colonel staring out the window. "Lost in thought, Higgs?" John asked.

The man turned and shook his head. "I'm worried about this operation of yours, John."

"It'll be dangerous, I'm aware of that."

"Frankly, I don't think you're bringing enough men." John's entire assault force consisted of sixty-seven men.

"I've thought the very same thing," John told him. "But there's a higher risk of being spotted if we bring in too many. Besides, I've got a couple tricks up my sleeve."

"Do you?"

"First off, I plan on arming as many of the prisoners as we can. I've already told you about having them scatter into the countryside to begin insurgency groups of their own, but before they do, we might be able to use their help in taking on the rest of the North Korean guards while we get everyone out."

Colonel Higgs cupped his hands behind his back. "I suppose my reservation stems from the fact that this'll be the first operation of its kind in the war to date."

"You're a man who knows his history," John said, sitting down.

"I'd like to think so."

"The Raid at Cabanatuan. That's what I'm using as a

model for this operation."

In January, 1945, a few hundred American and Filipino guerrillas had stormed a Japanese prisoner-of-war camp near Cabanatuan City. The raid had helped to free five hundred American POWs and was a resounding success.

John turned to Devon. "Any word from Moss?"

"Not yet, sir."

"The only issue still to be decided is how we'll get there. I was thinking a combination of horses and dirt bikes."

"Far too loud," Colonel Higgs said right away. "You don't want anything that'll risk giving away your position. If you have to go the bike route, then you're better off using mountain bikes. Even in a small town like Oneida, you're sure to find several. In fact, I see people riding them around every day." Higgs glanced down at the crude sketch John had drawn of the concentration camp. "So what exactly is your plan, John?"

"Six squads of nine men each." John pushed his finger down on key locations. "Alpha, Bravo, Charlie and Delta will take up positions on the north, south, east and west entrances to the camp. Echo will set up along 1st Street to block any enemy troops coming west from Jonesboro, while Foxtrot does the same for enemy forces coming in from the east."

Higgs was counting on his fingers. "That's only fifty-four out of sixty-seven men. What about the rest?"

"Eight of the remaining thirteen will be tasked with bringing up the QBZ-03 assault rifles and ammunition we stripped off the dead Chinese who attacked us. Three others will stay in the forest and guard the horses. Reese and Hoffman will be with them, acting as overwatch."

"Any intel on troop strengths in the area?" Higgs asked, studying the crude map.

"It's sketchy, but we've estimated the camp doesn't

have more than a couple hundred guards with perhaps the same number headquartered in Jonesboro itself."

Devon came to John's side. "Moss is back."

Chapter 29

John found him at the stables with the rest of the team who had accompanied Moss to Huntsville. Altogether, they'd managed to get twenty more horses of varying quality.

"That town's under occupation. We had a heck of a time evading a company of Chinese infantry that wanted us bad," Moss said. "And when all this is said and done," Moss told them, wearing a cocky grin, "I suggest you head down to Huntsville and personally thank those kind people."

John's brow furrowed. "Some of these horses look like they're on their last legs."

"Hey, beggars can't be choosers," Moss replied.

"We're still short rides for thirty-five men." Devon was nearby and John called him over. "Put together a team on the double to procure as many mountain bikes in town as you can. We'll need extra pumps and tires as well. Some of the stores may still have that kind of stock on their shelves."

Devon nodded and ran off.

Billy Ray showed up a short time later.

"Henry said you wanted to see me."

"I need a favor from you."

"Not Oak Ridge again."

Growing somber as he thought about Jerry, John shook his head. "I'll be happy if I never set foot there for the rest of my days. I need you to make another leaflet drop over Jonesboro concentration camp. Except it needs to be done tomorrow at exactly seven forty-five pm. Think you can do that?"

Billy Ray's eyes narrowed as he folded his thick forearms over his chest. "There something you ain't telling me?"

"I wish I could say more, but you'll just have to trust me on this. Men's lives will depend on you being there on time."

"Be there or be square, right?" Billy Ray spat.

"Right," John replied, shaking his hand. "Speak with my daughter Emma. She'll make sure you have the leaflets you need and if she doesn't have enough by then, you can drop blank pieces of paper."

"Blank pieces… This is getting weirder by the minute," Billy Ray said as he scratched the airplane grease off the tip of his nose.

John glanced at his watch. They were set to leave in two hours and there was still so much to do. Pushing the operation up would increase the challenge and the risks of pulling it off. Still, he couldn't help wonder whether they would get there in time.

He headed to the greenhouse to find Diane before he left. She was directing workers who were installing old street lights inside the greenhouse. Seeing his wife taking charge always gave him a warm feeling inside.

"If we weren't already married, I'd be tempted to drop down on one knee right now," he told her.

Diane used a hanky to dab the perspiration around her neck. The dirt in her hair matched the black streaks running down the sides of her cheeks. "Lucky for me your standards keep dropping."

"I see Ray's windmills are still going strong."

"We have enough juice now to power tools, and I've

heard rumors they're converting the old cookware manufacturer off Alberta Street into an armaments factory."

John folded his arms. "That's the plan. They've already started cutting up those destroyed Chinese tanks and fighting vehicles to use for making mortars and grenades."

"I can't imagine it'll make much difference, John. Other than to paint a giant target on our backs. Don't you think word of it will leak out from you-know-who?"

"That's part of what I wanted to talk to you about," John said. "We're going on an important mission right now. Something very few people in town know about."

"You're worried Phoenix might have caught wind?"

"We can't help but assume."

"So what do you want me to do?"

"Just keep an eye out for anyone acting suspicious."

"I'm already doing that," Diane said. "We all are. I was lying awake in bed last night, listening to you snore when I thought of something."

"I snore?"

She smiled. "Of course you do, but that isn't the important part. I think I know a way to find our mole. Strategic misinformation."

John took a step back. "That's a mouthful, even for you."

Diane grinned and swatted his shoulder. "It means you purposely let an important secret slip out to the people at the top of your suspect list, only each person is told a slightly different version. The enemy's reaction should reveal which of the stories was leaked and by whom."

"Sounds complicated, but I like it," he told her, dropping down on one knee.

"Oh, stop it," she said, yanking on his arm to stand him up. "I don't know what foolhardy mission you're heading on this time, but whenever you leave I keep hoping I'll see you return with Gregory."

John pulled her into a hug, feeling the beat of her heart as he pressed her into him. "I hope so too. Until then, pray that he be kept safe."

When John finally returned to the stables, his men were prepped and ready to leave. The weight of their assault rifles, ammunition, and AT-4 anti-tank rockets as well as food and water was at the upper limit of what they could carry. But by far the heaviest load was the extra weapons they planned on handing out to the prisoners they freed.

As they left Oneida for the second time in so many days—an ungainly procession of soldiers on horses and bikes—John hoped that Diane would pray for them as well.

Chapter 30

Brandon's heart was hammering in his chest as he made his way to the camp commandant's headquarters. The building lay just up ahead, a squat, single-story structure identical to the dark brown barracks set in endless rows within the enclosure. The only visible difference was the giant decal of the red Communist star inside a white circle on the side of the building, a symbol also emblazoned on the uniforms of every North Korean prison guard.

As terrifying as what Brandon was about to do was, he wouldn't be able to live with himself if anything happened to Gregory. The responsibility he felt for his younger friend went far beyond their difference in age. Right or wrong, Gregory had opted out of the escape plan, preferring to stay behind and await the rescue he believed was on its way. How could Brandon show his face in Oneida again with the knowledge he'd done nothing to stop Gregory's execution, even if such a move would result in his own torture and death?

Two guards stood at attention on either side of the entrance to the headquarters. As Brandon drew near, they raised their weapons and shouted perhaps the only English word they knew.

"Halt!"

He did as they said, raising his hands above his head.

The fear on his face must have been obvious because the guards hadn't shot him.

"I need to see the commandant," he told them.

They squinted and shook their heads.

Brandon didn't think they understood and repeated his request.

One of the guards pulled his hand off the hand grip and waved Brandon away. Within a few seconds they would begin shooting.

Just then, Ellis emerged from the commandant's office. "Get outta here, kid, unless you have some kind of death wish."

"Tell them I need to speak with the commandant."

He laughed. "I'm a prisoner here just as much as you are. I don't tell these folks anything."

"They're about to execute an innocent boy. He wasn't part of the escape plan, I was."

Ellis's jaw fell open. "Okay, wait right here and don't move a muscle." He disappeared inside. After a few agonizing minutes, he returned.

"Looks like you got your wish."

Brandon was waved forward and quickly frisked for weapons by the two guards. Afterward, they led him into a modest room. On his left was a red antique couch with carved lion's-paw feet. At the far end sat a simple oak desk and stretched on the wall behind that was a giant map of the United States. A blood-red line had been drawn from left to right through the middle of the country. To the south were Chinese and North Korean flags. To the north of the red line was a Russian flag and spread throughout the entire map were tiny yellow stars. One, often two per state. Were these the locations of enemy bases and strong points?

The two guards nudged him with the butts of their rifles as a door at the far end of the room opened and in walked the commandant.

He was dressed in an olive-green officer's uniform, his chest bursting with decorations and ribbons. He removed his hat and laid it on the desk, pushing back his dark, thinning hair with one hand. A short man with harsh features, he looked unassuming.

Could this be the same man responsible for siccing his German Shepherds on disobedient prisoners?

"You have thirty second," the commandant said in broken English.

Brandon could feel the artery in his neck thumping wildly. "Your men have arrested the wrong person. Gregory Mack was pulled off the fields earlier and charged with plotting to escape and I know for a fact that he's innocent."

The commandant paused, glaring at Brandon as though an alien life form were standing before him. "Is that all?"

"I know what I'm telling you," Brandon said, "because I'm the one who's guilty, not him."

The commandant raised an eyebrow. "You know what this will mean for you?"

Brandon nodded. "It means you should take me instead."

"Very brave…" The commandant waited. "Brandon, is it?"

He nodded.

"Very brave or very foolish? Which do you think?"

"Maybe both," Brandon said, unsure.

"I think you are right. I saw when I came in you were looking at the map behind me."

"Yes, I was wondering what the stars meant."

The commandant glanced back over his shoulder.

"They represent how lucky you are."

"I don't understand."

"I am a fair man, Brandon. But only when prisoners

obey my commands. When they don't I become angry. Each of those stars is a political prison camp and in many of them, the work done by the prisoners is much more brutal, as are the punishments." He pointed to the middle of the map. "This one here was built next to a coal mine in the state you once called Kansas, but is now Huang-Shi province. Nearly a hundred die there every day. I receive many letters from the commandant there asking for fresh laborers. Just as I receive requests from the front for men of eligible age for forced conscription."

Brandon swallowed hard.

"Yes, even you hard-headed Americans can be taught to see the folly of resisting." The commandant shouted something in Korean and the two guards stormed into the room, took Brandon by the arms and began dragging him away.

"What about Gregory?" he shouted, but the commandant didn't answer.

Chapter 31

"You push that horse any harder," Reese told John, "and it's liable to keel over."

John glanced down and saw his horse breathing hard and pulled back on the reins. Getting there a tad bit later was better than not getting there at all. Besides, John would make do by going over the battle plan in his head one more time.

Reese pulled up alongside him, bouncing in his saddle. On the left collar of the sniper's fatigues was a white feather.

"I've been meaning to ask you about that," John said, pointing.

Reese glanced down. "It's my Carlos Hathcock."

"Your what?"

"One of the greatest snipers our country's ever produced. Used to wear a white feather in the band of his hat. Was his trademark. Grew up a country boy from Arkansas shooting small game and went on to rack up ninety-three confirmed kills in Vietnam."

John agreed that was an impressive number.

"You might not know this," Reese went on, fishing one of his horrible-smelling cigarettes out of a squished pack, "but during that war, kills could only be confirmed by an officer. That is, someone other than the sniper's spotter. Guess it was designed to stop hotshots from padding their stats. Anyway, Hathcock swore that ninety-three was far too low. Said the real number was somewhere in the neighborhood of three to four hundred enemies killed."

John's eyebrows rose.

"That's right. Commies even put a thirty-thousand-dollar bounty on his head. And you can imagine with a contract like that, the Viet Cong and NVA snipers were pouring in from the north intent on getting a hold of that feather."

"Did they get him?"

"Oh, they tried," Reese said with a smile. "Closest they got was a mysterious sniper who went by the code name Cobra. He'd already killed a bunch of Marines in an effort to draw Hathcock out. For several days the two enemies stalked one another. Both of them made narrow escapes as one would close in on the other. Then one day, Hathcock found some disturbed brush and spotted a trail through an open field. He set himself up with his back to the sun."

"To keep the light out of his eyes," John said. "Smart man."

"Not only that, but in those days they still had scopes that reflected shards of sunlight. After scanning for a few minutes, Hathcock spotted a twinkle in the bush, swung his rifle around and fired right at it. When they crossed over they found the Cobra dead. Shot through the lens of his own scope."

"No way."

"No joke. A one-in-a-million shot that meant the Cobra had them in his sights. If Hathcock had waited a split second longer, he might have been the one dead." Reese touched the white feather pin on his collar. "Since I heard that story, I've always carried this with me. Call it a good-luck charm."

John turned back to the trail, praying Reese's luck would help get them there in time.

Chapter 32

A short time later, the prisoner population was assembled inside the courtyard in order to witness the latest batch of executions. After Brandon's talk with the commandant, he hadn't been whisked away to join Dixon, Gregory and the others condemned to die. Instead he'd been returned to the barracks, where he'd sat weeping while he stared at Gregory's empty bunk.

Now, he stood in formation with the other prisoners, numb with pain. On some level, walking to the commandant's office had felt like the slow march to the electric chair. The whole time the gnawing fear that his actions might end with his own death had never gone away, but in a way only a condemned prisoner could understand, he'd somehow made peace with the idea.

Of course, looking back, the chances that he might have been lined up and bayoneted alongside Gregory were just as good. And if that had happened, then what would he have accomplished? Perhaps this was why the commandant had asked if he was brave or foolish. Even now, Brandon wasn't sure which was the right answer. If there was anything he'd learned from John, it was that doing something, anything, was often better than doing nothing at all.

The prisoners slated for execution were led out in a long ragged line. They were nearly the entire group Dixon had put together. Even with the black bags over their heads, Brandon could still see Dixon and Gregory bringing up the rear. The sight sucked the moisture right out of his mouth.

The guards halted the condemned and turned them to face the crowd. Soon the bayoneting would start and Brandon was sure the sight of his friends being killed would make him physically sick.

The pug-faced guard, Lee Kun-Hee, moved to the far end, steadying his rifle before plunging the bayonet into the first prisoner. They shrieked in agony before collapsing to the ground. On he went, working his way down the line as the commandant stood nearby watching.

When he arrived at Dixon, Brandon felt the sudden urge to scream out, to say something in protest at the cruel indignity of it all. But Brandon didn't get a chance to say a word before Dixon shouted, "Long live America."

The prisoners erupted with cheers just as Pug Face thrust his blade into Dixon's belly. The soldier let out a moan and fell to his knees. Other guards fired warning shots into the air to regain control.

A second jab from Pug Face ended it and Dixon slumped to the ground. Angry tears welled up behind Brandon's eyes, but he knew the worst was yet to come.

With Dixon and the others dead, Pug Face stood before Gregory. Once again he pulled back his rifle and Brandon felt the air catch in his throat.

A shout in Korean from the commandant made Pug Face freeze in mid thrust, the blade inches from Gregory's stomach.

"It has come to my attention this boy was wrongfully accused," the commandant said, addressing the crowd himself this time. "I hereby release him back into the general population. Let none of you think that I am an unfair and unjust man."

The prisoners stood speechless. Even Brandon didn't know what to say. Had his bold and dangerous move to plead for Gregory's life actually paid off?

Reluctantly, Pug Face removed the hood and cut the ropes that bound Gregory's hands. For a moment the boy stood confused until the guard pushed him forward, sending him back toward the line of prisoners.

The commandant then issued an order in Korean and immediately, the guards pushed their way through the deep rows of prisoners, pulling out several males in their teens and twenties. The crowd split as Brandon spotted Pug Face heading in his direction, pushing aside prisoners as he came. A second later, the ugly guard grabbed him by the arm and yanked him out to stand with the others.

This was it. This was where he and dozens of others would be executed in Gregory's place. The price for saving his young friend hadn't only been his own life. It had cost the lives of everyone else standing alongside him.

But Brandon wasn't entirely right. This wasn't an execution. Instead, the commandant lined the men up and paced before them.

"From this moment on," he told them, "you lucky few are conscripts in the People's Liberation Army. First you will be sent for training. Afterward you will be shipped to the front. Fraternity, dexterity, sincerity. These are the virtues you will acquire. May you make the Communist Party and the Eastern Alliance proud."

Brandon couldn't believe what he was hearing. Conscripted into the Chinese army. He knew the

Germans had done the same to the Russians, Bulgarians and others after conquering their lands during World War Two, a move that was particularly sinister since men on the battlefield, unwilling as they might be, tended to fight for their own survival, even if that meant firing on their own people.

Moments before they were marched away, the commandant gave them one final warning. "If any of you fail to do your duty to the fullest, hundreds here will be executed in punishment."

With that stark threat ringing in his ears, Brandon caught sight of Gregory in the line of prisoners. He was crying and both of them knew this would be the last time they would see each other.

Chapter 33

Back in Oneida, only a handful of the workers repairing the greenhouse were present when dusk arrived. Diane gripped the hammer and drove a nail into a table joint with three whacks. Once finished, this would be one of several platforms lining the interior of the greenhouse.

Diane paused to scan the darkening sky, wondering where the members of her family were at this very moment. Emma was in the basement struggling against that printing press. Over the last few days she'd found something of a calling, cranking out those propaganda leaflets by the hundreds. So long as she held onto the hope that Brandon and Gregory would return, Diane knew her daughter could keep herself together.

Diane hadn't been speaking metaphorically about praying for Gregory and Brandon's safe return when she and John had last spoken. The act of stopping throughout the day to give thanks and beg for their protection had become a ritual in and of itself. Which led her to the final member of her family, John. He was gone again doing his part and she couldn't fault him for that, although the selfish side of her wondered why the responsibility always seemed to fall on his shoulders. Or maybe a more accurate way of looking at it was why John seemed to always take so much on himself.

In the days since they first arrived in Oneida, it seemed that the Mack family had seen less and less of each other. Much of that had to do with the difficult circumstances they were in as the community struggled not only to survive but to thrive in a new world that wanted nothing more than to destroy them. And Diane wasn't simply talking about the Chinese. Disease, starvation, exposure were only three of a million ways their surroundings conspired against them.

Hands on her hips, a trickle of sweat running down her back, Diane began to turn her attention back to the table when something drew her attention. Past the greenhouse and the twin windmills chopping lazily at the air above her, a thin figure in dark jeans and a black hoodie stepped into the woodlands that ran next to the high school. Diane stood, staring for a moment, wondering if her mind was playing tricks on her. Whoever it was had what looked like a piece of paper in his hand, which he folded as he disappeared. But what struck her as odd wasn't merely that the man's hoodie was pulled up over his head on such a warm evening, it was that he was heading toward the woods on the edge of town. Most citizens steered clear of the forest, especially when dusk drew near. A few miles away lay the Chinese lines. Sure, there were a handful of American troops positioned at key sections along the perimeter, but they couldn't watch the whole area at once.

Diane picked up the hammer and was about to go back to work when she stopped and let it fall to the ground. The Colt .45 in the holster on her hip gave her a feeling of confidence and John's final words to keep an eye out helped to infuse her with a sense of obligation. She turned to one of the workers nearby, a man in his fifties named Stew who wore a long beard and tie-dye t-shirt. "Did you see that?" she asked, pointing toward the forest's edge.

Stew glanced up, looking tired and more than a little impatient. "Right now all I see is my bed."

There was normally a pair of guards patrolling the area, but right now she didn't see them. "Listen, I'm going to check something out. Just keep an eye out for the patrol and send them over my way. Will you do that?"

Stew shrugged. "Sure."

Making her way toward the spot where she'd seen the dark figure disappear, Diane felt her chest tighten. Having a gun didn't always do a whole lot to ease one's mind when you were on the cusp of entering a dark area, a feeling only made worse when you were pursuing someone who might be up to no good.

Her holster was an old tan leather World War Two replica and she unsnapped the flap, curling her fingers around the pistol grip. She arrived at the treeline, keeping low, giving her eyes a moment to adjust. The sound of snapping twigs and crunching leaves nearby made her anxiety spike.

Heart hammering in her neck, she crept into the shadow cast by the leaves overhead, not wanting to be outlined by standing in the dying light. Still, she saw nothing. Then slowly, fuzzy shapes began to take on solid form as her eyes grew accustomed to the lack of proper light. Crouched down behind a maple tree, she spotted the shadow of a man going from left to right. He was twenty yards away, crossing in front of her on their way back toward town. Soon he emerged from the woods empty-handed.

What about the piece of paper she'd seen him carrying? Had he slipped it into a pocket? Or had he left it behind for someone else to find?

But the thought which drowned out all others was that she suddenly knew who she was looking at: Phoenix.

Diane drew her pistol and hurried out of the woods,

stumbling through brush and over fallen branches. As soon as she reached the clearing, she flicked off the safety on her .45 and leveled it at the figure in dark clothing who was walking away.

"Stop right there," she shouted.

The figure hesitated, but kept on going.

Diane broke into a quick jog, her pistol at the low ready, finger along the barrel just off the trigger.

The figure turned and glanced back and this was the first clear sight she caught of him. He appeared thin and malnourished. But the fear blooming on his face told her right away she had the right man. Only someone up to no good would be nervous when asked to stop. Guilty men also didn't break into a run and that was exactly what he did.

Diane swore and tore after him. The temptation to fire was strong, but if she was right and this was indeed Phoenix, then they would need to take him alive.

His clothes rippled on his narrow frame. His pants were sliding down, forcing him to hold his waistband as he fled.

"This is your last warning," she shouted as she leveled her pistol and fired a warning shot in the air.

A second later, the suspect ducked in through the doorway of a nearby building.

Nearby a group of civilians gathering chunks of steel from a pile of debris stopped and stared at her with startled apprehension.

"He went in there," one of them, said pointing.

She spotted one of Colonel Higgs' men heading this way, his M4 clutched in both hands.

"Soldier, I need your help clearing this building," she told him. "We've got someone inside who may be a Chinese agent."

"Let me go in first, Mrs. Mack," he said, recognizing her. The soldier reached into a pouch and attached a tactical flashlight onto his rifle.

She followed him inside, sweeping the rooms with him as best she could. She had never been trained for this. When he entered a room from the left, she covered the right angle. Part of it was common sense, but no doubt her lack of experience meant she was making mistakes. Hopefully mistakes that wouldn't get them killed. With the bottom floor cleared, the two made their way upstairs.

"Oneida security," the soldier shouted, swinging his flashlight rapidly from one corner to the next. "There's no use resisting."

They were in what was once the office for a tractor rental company. Desks in each room showcased computers that were as dead as the people who'd used them probably were.

The door of the final office bore the name Timothy Simmons and both Diane and the soldier entered cautiously. Unless the assailant had somehow managed to dematerialize like they did on those sci-fi shows on TV, then he was in this room.

The soldier pointed to the closet behind the desk. Framed pictures with a pair of toothless kids and a plain-looking woman sat by on the window ledge, collecting dust.

Closing his hand around the closet door handle, the soldier drew in a deep breath, his M4 steadied in his other hand.

He jerked it open and that was when the man inside held up his hands, his eyes wide and filled with primal fear.

The soldier grabbed him by the hoodie and yanked him out onto his face. Diane helped place and tighten zip ties around his wrists before both of them lifted the man to his feet and all at once she recognized the gaunt and frightened face staring back at her.

It was David Newbury.

Chapter 34

Despite the heavy load of weapons and supplies the Rough Riders brought with them, John's guerrilla force made great time. They reached the wood line facing the Jonesboro concentration camp late on the second day at just after 1700 hours.

John had pushed his horse and many of his men to near their breaking point in his determination to arrive as quickly as possible. Only warnings from Reese that John's horse might drop dead had made him pull back.

Now in place, they sat and waited for the sun to dip beyond the horizon. At precisely 1945, John would give the order for his men to crawl into position for the main assault. About five hundred yards to the north Delta, Echo and Foxtrot squads were concealed in the forest next to the road. John kept in touch with each of his six squads with encrypted military-grade PRC-17 walkie-talkies, although he'd given his men instructions to maintain radio silence unless it was absolutely necessary.

When the signal was given, Delta and Echo would set up blocking positions along the east and west approaches on 1st Street while Foxtrot would face the camp's front entrance. Their role wasn't to storm in via the most likely avenue of approach, but rather to draw North Korean soldiers away from the main battle. Foxtrot's secondary mission was to provide extra support to Delta and Echo on their flanks should the enemy reinforcements come in heavier than expected.

The main assault on the eastern side would come from John's own squad, Alpha. Bravo and Charlie would attack the southern and western fence lines respectively. In sniper support was Reese and a soldier with the 101st named Hoffman. The crack of their rifles taking out the first tower guards would be the signal to attack.

John swept the camp perimeter with his binoculars. Beside him, Reese did the same with the scope of his Remington 700. Guards in groups of twos and threes were visible walking outside the fence. Visibility inside the camp was obstructed by the rows of barracks and other buildings. But David Newbury had mentioned a courtyard and that executions sometimes took place there, although at this point it was impossible to see what was going on. The place seemed to be quiet, which was good. Launching the assault when the prisoners were out in the open would only have complicated the operation and put American lives at risk.

Behind him, the three squads of Rough Riders kept busy checking their weapons and gear. He took that opportunity to reach into his wallet for a picture of Gregory, taken for his high-school yearbook. His hair was short and turned up slightly at the front, a reference to some pop star he'd been trying to emulate. John stared at it for a long time before tucking it away. There was still work to do.

His mind shifted to the tools of his trade. As always, John carried his S&W along with his trusty AR-15. Many of the men with him used their standard-issue M4s, mostly because that was what they knew best. A few outliers opted for AK-47s and 74s.

Then at 1942 John caught the sound of a prop plane heading toward them from the east.

He, Reese and Moss all shared a knowing look.

Bringing the walkie to his lips, John depressed the

actuator and spoke. "Prepare to move out on my signal."

The sound of the plane's engine grew louder until the underbelly streaked overhead, cutting through the weakening light. Although it was sporting Chinese air force colors, John knew right away Billy Ray had kept his word. The Cessna barrelled toward the camp right as John gave the order for his men to break cover and crawl into position.

Chapter 35

The Cessna came in low and fast and pulled up right as it reached the fence line. Bundles of leaflets streamed from the open back door as Billy Ray passed over the camp. It was important that he spread the papers out as far as possible. The plane would not only serve as a distraction, pulling the guards' eyes off the perimeter, it should also suck up manpower as they scrambled to collect the falling American propaganda before it landed in the prisoners' hands.

From their concealed position, Reese and Hoffman kept an eye on the guards in the tower, ready to warn the squads whenever they risked being seen. Alpha, Bravo and Charlie squads emerged from the woods, keeping low to the ground, but not crawling. The low crawl they would save for once they were closer to the camp. Although they weren't visible from here, John knew Delta, Echo and Foxtrot on his right were doing the same. This was the trickiest stage of the operation, getting his men across an open field and into position for the attack without being spotted.

Their first objective was the drainage ditches a hundred yards away which ran parallel to both the eastern and southern fence lines.

"I got enemy eyes looking your way," Reese said calmly over the walkie.

John, out front, patted the empty air by his hip, an

order for his men to go prone. They dropped at once and froze.

A handful of nerve-racking seconds passed.

The Cessna was now starting to take fire and Billy Ray dumped the rest of the leaflets and tipped his wings into a sharp turn toward the east.

Come on, John thought, feeling the anxiety creeping up his legs. *We don't have time for this.*

Inside the camp, the guards were already busy collecting the papers. As John had hoped, even the perimeter guards had run back in to help their comrades.

"All clear," Reese said at last.

John gave the signal and the three squads were back on their feet, their boots clomping over uneven ground.

When they reached the drainage ditch, Bravo and Charlie dropped into it, moving south until they found the intersecting ditch. This would hopefully allow them to approach the southern and western gates without being detected.

The lack of equipment had meant only the squad leaders had a walkie and an earpiece. Once Charlie climbed out of the depression, John would move the men of Alpha to within three hundred feet. In these last few crucial moments, timing and precision would mean everything.

For now they would keep low and rely on Reese to keep an eye out for any sentries who might wander too close. A quick check in with Delta, Echo and Foxtrot informed him they were making good progress. Delta was already blocking the eastern approach to the camp. The other two were still en route to their destination.

"So far, so good," Moss said, encouraged. In the dimming light, the black camo paint on everyone's faces made it hard to see anything but the whites of their eyes.

John poked his head up and peered through his

binoculars. The North Koreans had started a bonfire in the middle of the camp where soldiers were burning handfuls of leaflets at a time.

"How long do you think before they finish cleaning up?" Moss asked, checking his rifle for the millionth time.

"Hard to say," John replied. Nervousness didn't turn him into a chatterbox the same way it did Moss. Far from trying to banish the anxiety, John felt it was often the very thing which kept him fully alert and on his toes.

Then came messages from Bravo, Echo and Foxtrot. They were all in position. That only left Charlie, which wasn't a huge surprise, since they had the most ground to cover.

John checked the time and saw that it was nearly 20:00.

Then came the sound of gunfire and everyone in Alpha perked up at once.

"Those are AKs," Moss said, worried.

A half-second later came the sound of the American M4s answering back. John didn't need to be told that Charlie was taking fire and possibly pinned down in open terrain. More than that, Charlie's squad leader wasn't radioing in, which meant he might have been wounded or killed.

John pulled out a stopwatch strung around his neck and started the countdown. If the attack on the truck depot was anything to go by, then they could expect Chinese and North Korean reinforcements from Jonesboro to show up within the next twenty minutes. Getting on the walkie to Reese, John sent his sniper a single message. "Go to work."

Chapter 36

John and his men stormed out of the drainage ditch to the crack of Reese's Remington 700. The round hit the tower guard just below the throat, spraying the wooden beam behind him with blood.

A second sniper shot rang out, this time from Hoffman killing another tower guard. Alpha was now charging the eastern gate at a full run, pausing here and there to fire. From the drainage ditch, Benson, their machine gunner, laid down suppressing fire with his M249. Along with Reese's surgical strikes, the supporting fire from his weapon would keep the enemy's heads pinned down, allowing John and his men to reach the gate without being cut down.

Soon chaos was erupting in every direction as each squad engaged the North Korean guards. For their part, the enemy soldiers seemed to be fighting back with equal determination. A small satchel charge carried by Alpha's explosives expert, Specialist Heller, would blow the gate open once they got close.

Two shots whistled past John's right ear. He dropped into a prone position and made a quick scan for the threat. A guard ducking behind a wooden building poked his head out and fired again. Rounds thudded into the ground, kicking up puffs of dirt. John peered through the scope of his AR, acquired the edge of the structure the guard kept popping out from behind and

waited. He didn't have to wait long. Out came the man's head, his
facial features tense with fear. John squeezed the trigger and the soldier's head snapped back before his body fell somewhere out of sight.

Pushing back onto this feet, John spotted Heller and three other men from Alpha already at the gate, prepping the charge.

"Cover on eastern gate," John radioed to Reese and Hoffman.

"On it," came the reply.

When the charge was set, Heller and the others pulled back and dropped to the ground.

A second later, the satchel detonated with such force it tossed the gate twenty feet into the air, where it landed on an unsuspecting guard.

Heller looked surprised and elated. "Hole in one."

"Good job," John said, before he got on the walkie and ordered the men tasked with carrying the QBZ-03s to come forward. The minute those prisoners were freed, he wanted to arm as many of them as he could.

With that done, Alpha surged forward and into the camp. If everything had gone smoothly on Bravo's end, he expected to meet them somewhere in the center of camp. As for Charlie, he could only hope he would see them there too.

Chapter 37

Half-dressed North Korean troops stormed from their military barracks in the center of camp directly into the sights of John and his men. Dropping down to one knee, John and the other members of Alpha opened fire, mowing them down in a hail of bullets. Each team member knew their role and which angle to cover as the group pushed forward. When Bravo showed up a moment later, pouring in fire from the south, the North Koreans' will to fight seemed to dissolve entirely. Many enemy soldiers ran for the front gate where they were met by Echo and quickly eliminated.

John met up with Bravo's squad leader, a young, quiet soldier named Gardner. "Any word from Charlie?" John asked, hopeful.

Working a piece of chewing tobacco under his bottom lip, Gardner spat on the ground. "Not yet, sir."

Staring down the path that looked onto the western gate, John saw that it hadn't been blown. That meant Charlie was still out there, wounded or possibly KIA. "All right, let's proceed with the mission. We can check on them once we free these prisoners."

Sporadic gunfire signaled pockets of enemy soldiers still holding out. John checked his stopwatch. Ten minutes had already gone by. They would need to hurry before reinforcements arrived.

Alpha and Bravo broke into nine groups of two men each in order to break open the prisoner barracks doors and let people out.

The American soldiers bringing up the QBZ-03s entered through the eastern gate and set themselves up in the courtyard.

John reached into his back pocket and came out with the picture of Gregory. The edges were frayed and the image wasn't terribly recent, but he hoped that someone here would be able to help John find him.

He and Moss kicked in the door to the nearest prison barracks and went in, weapons drawn.

"We're Americans," John shouted to rows of empty bunk beds. "And we're here to free you." For a moment, his heart stuttered in his chest. The place was empty. Had the people inside already been shipped somewhere else, or worse, had they been killed?

Slowly a frightened woman emerged from behind one of the beds. That was when it dawned on him. They didn't trust him—probably thought this was some sort of North Korean mind game designed to find out who'd jump at the chance to escape and then execute them on the spot.

"Do I need to start singing a Britney Spears song for you people to do as I say? You've got one chance to get out of here and this is it."

Suddenly more heads popped up and the room that had seemed empty at first was now filled with women in tattered clothing rushing for the door. They seemed weak and befuddled, but John hoped they knew this was only the beginning. He stood by the door as Moss went to the back of the barracks, flushing out any resisters. Outside, the troops who'd brought the weapons ushered the prisoners into the courtyard.

The picture of his son was in John's hand, illuminated by the glow of his tactical light. "Do any of you know my son? His name is Gregory."

Several ran past in a hurry, glancing quickly and shaking their heads.

"I just need to know which barracks he's in."

An older woman in her late sixties or early seventies with stringy silver hair studied the picture before grinning. "I've seen him before. Sweet boy."

"Where can I find him?"

The expression on her thin face shifted. "I think they killed him."

John tried to hide the devastation that must have clearly been visible, choking back the sudden urge to vomit.

"I'm so sorry."

John nodded, covering his mouth. From what seemed like a great distance, he heard the other squad leaders report back over the radio that the prisoners were being assembled in the courtyard and the most able-bodied among them armed. John's head was still reeling when another message came through, this one from Foxtrot.

"Colonel, we've got a large force incoming. At least battalion strength and backed up by ZBD-08 Infantry fighting vehicles."

The enemy counterattack had come sooner than he expected.

Chapter 38

"Echo," John called over the walkie, stuffing staggering grief down as far as it would go. "Do you copy?"

"Loud and clear," the team leader reported back.

"Move your men west to support Foxtrot. There's a large enemy force coming your way. Could be as many as eight hundred men supported by armor. Use your AT-4s and if it gets too hot, fall back to the prison camp."

"Roger that."

John ordered Reese and Hoffman to redeploy north along the tree line so they could get a clear field of fire down 1st Street.

At this rate, they would never be able to get everyone out in time. John had known that going in, so he ordered women, children and anyone too weakened by starvation to fight to head toward the St. Francis reserve. At least there they could hide and stay safe for the time being. If the worst happened and the enemy overran the prison, at least they might have a chance of escape.

Moss ran up to him. "I just ran into what's left of Charlie. Found them straggling in through the southern gate. Said they got spotted and pinned down after their team leader was killed. Half of them didn't make it."

It could have been much worse. "Have some of the armed prisoners take over liberating the barracks and handing out weapons," John told his number two. "We're nearly out of time. Grab what you can off of dead guards if need be. And there must be an armory in here somewhere. Find it."

"Will do," Moss said, about to run off. "What about the prisoners we've already equipped?"

"Get them into the towers along the northwestern wall to help Foxtrot and Echo. I'll take what's left of Alpha, Bravo and Charlie out the western gate and see if we can't flank these guys and catch them in a pincer."

Moss laughed. "Heinz Guderian would be proud to hear you say that."

He was referring to the founder of the German *blitzkrieg*, a tactic used to great effect during World War Two to encircle and destroy large enemy formations.

By the time John assembled the remaining squad members and charged out the western gates, reports were already coming in from Foxtrot that the enemy was approaching the kill zone. A cornfield up ahead would offer the concealment they needed to get within striking range. They reached a depression in the terrain which in the rapidly fading light John assumed was another drainage ditch. But as they drew closer they saw that it was far too deep and wide to be a ditch. The smell of lye became strong, almost overpowering as the beams of their tactical lights illuminated a pit filled with hundreds of bodies. For a moment, the men stood transfixed, unable to look away and struggling to process the sight before them.

"What the heck is this?" Heller, Alpha's explosives expert, asked.

John switched his light off, feeling the rage surging up his throat like bile. "A mass grave," he answered. "And it's filled with dead Americans."

Chapter 39

After circling around the mass grave, they entered the cornfield and John was thankful to have the smell of decaying bodies replaced with that of damp earth. A violent explosion sounded up ahead as the trap sprang. Echo and Foxtrot were no doubt pouring anti-tank rockets and gunfire into the kill zone. His own men were deployed in a line-abreast formation as they pushed through the rows of cornstalks before them.

A few more meters and they would reach the clearing. Just then John's radio crackled to life.

"Colonel, we found the armory," Moss reported. "She's filled with lots of small arms and grenades."

"Good news," John replied, pulling the charging handle on his AR and swinging his rifle into the low ready position.

"Well, if you liked that, then you're going to love this."

"Spit it out, Moss, there's no time for cuteness."

"We found an 81mm mortar."

John smiled. "You're right, I do love it. Set it up on the double. I'll correct your round placement. Just remember that everything you send downrange will be danger close."

The firefight was still going strong by the time John and the rest of the men reached the edge of the cornfield. The roadway was filled with enemy soldiers. To the right, a handful of infantry fighting vehicles burned on the road. Squatting behind them were clumps of North Korean soldiers, taking cover. Two platoon-sized reinforcements moved along the opposite side of the road and John called for his men to open fire.

Rounds peppered the unsuspecting enemy soldiers, tearing many of them to pieces. Several tried to fall back into the cornfield on the north side of the road and were cut down. The incoming rounds thudded into men and stalks of corn alike, sending them both tumbling to the ground as though a giant scythe had chopped them at the knee.

Some of the enemy soldiers who made it into the field began returning fire. Bullets whizzed by inches from John's head, striking ears of corn nearby.

Even over the sound of battle John caught the distant crack of Reese's sniper rifle and saw the devastating effects first-hand as the rounds found their mark, killing one and sometimes two soldiers at a time. A group of the enemy peeled away from the main force on the road and entered the cornfield to the left of John's position.

"Bravo," John shouted over the radio. "We've got company along our left flank. Have your men form a line along to intercept them."

"Will do," Gardner, the team leader, replied.

That was when the first mortar round came whistling overhead and slammed into the cornfield fifty yards in front of them. John signalled Moss on the radio.

"Left thirty, drop ten," he said.

"Left thirty, drop ten," Moss repeated.

Another round came sailing over and exploded ten yards into the cornfield, sending plants and men flying into the air.

"Great shot," John called back. "Adjust fire. Left ten. Drop five."

The North Korean soldiers firing at John and the other Americans seemed oblivious that the mortar team was zeroing in on their position. That was the difference between experienced troops and the kind who'd just come out of basic training.

The next mortar was loud as it came whistling in.

"Heads down," John shouted, not wanting his men to take any shrapnel from so close a strike.

The mortar round struck the edge of the field, churning up soil and men in a giant explosion.

"Heavy contact," Bravo's team leader shouted over the radio. "Need reinforcements."

John shifted what was left of Charlie over to help out while his own men in Alpha continued firing toward the road.

From the rear of their position came the sound of men charging through the cornfield. John turned, his weapon poised, just in time to see skinny men draped in tattered clothing wielding AKs and QBZ-03s. They were prisoners who had likely stripped weapons from the arsenal and were thirsty for revenge. They streamed past John's men without any concern for their own personal safety. Alpha held their fire as they ran by, the prisoners letting loose with what sounded like the rebel yell as they opened up on a terrified enemy.

John radioed Moss and his mortar team to stand down. For their part, the North Koreans broke and ran in every direction. Many were shot in the back as they tried to flee. Without a doubt, this went against John's sense of honour and dignity on the battlefield. But in this kind of war, where you were fighting for your very way of life, there wasn't any room for mercy. As he had said before during that meeting in Oneida, John's Rough Riders weren't going to be like Jeb Stuart's cavalry. They were Bloody Bill Anderson's men reborn.

With the enemy broken and running back toward

Jonesboro, John pulled his men together and made a quick tally of Alpha, Bravo and Charlie's losses. Five killed and six with mostly minor wounds. They moved over the battlefield, finishing off the enemy wounded and collecting as much gear as they could. Even members of Foxtrot and Echo came to help. It wouldn't be long before an even bigger force showed up and that meant they needed to leave and fast.

They headed back toward the prison, carrying the men who'd lost their lives, along with the plundered gear.

"What about those yahoos who ran off chasing the North Koreans?" Heller asked, not entirely able to hide his amusement.

"With no way to call them back," John said, "I guess we'll just have to let them have their fun and hope they don't get themselves killed."

"Colonel," Moss said over the radio, "I think you better come quick."

Chapter 40

When John and his men reached the camp, they found Moss and a handful of others waiting for them at the mouth of the western gate. His second-in-command had his arm around a young prisoner in rags, the boy's cheeks and eye sockets sunken with hunger. But it was only when John got to within a few feet that he recognized his son.

In spite of his weakened condition, Gregory ran into his father's arms. John clutched him tightly, weeping with disbelief, his hands running over ribs that were never meant to protrude so far.

"I was told you were dead," John said, unable to stop squeezing. Part of him wondered if this was real or some cruel hallucination.

"It was Brandon," Gregory replied in a low voice. His chestnut hair was long now and in his face. "He offered to take my place and was taken away."

"Taken away to where?" John asked, checking his son for wounds.

"To fight for the Chinese."

They'd conscripted him. It was an inevitable move that had happened countless times throughout history as conquering armies sought to replace depleted manpower. Often that took the form of slave labour camps, like the one they had just liberated. But even the Nazi army had raised troops to fight for its cause in France, Norway and a host of other countries that would surprise many.

"Don't worry, son," John said. "We'll find him and get him back." John couldn't help thinking about Emma and how devastated she would be by the news.

"We don't have long," Moss reminded him gently. "Several groups of prisoners have already fled into the countryside."

John looked up, remembering what he'd seen on the way to the cornfield.

"We're not done yet. I want every North Korean you can find assembled in the courtyard within five minutes."

"Already done, boss," Moss replied.

John grinned and clapped him on the back as they headed in that direction.

When they arrived, they found a dozen officers tied to poles. According to Gregory, these men had executed Dixon and countless others. Hearing that made John pause. His time in Iraq and warzones around the world continued to torture him to this very day. He couldn't imagine what his son had seen in this terrible place and how that might impact him down the road.

"Where are the rest of the guards?" John asked.

Moss shook his head with disgust. "They're all dead. Fought to the last man or shot in the back trying to run away. Most of these clowns we found hiding under desks or in crawl spaces." He pointed to a small group of Americans huddled together with the remaining North Korean guards. "And I don't have words for these ones. Prisoners tell me they're American collaborators."

John shook his head. "What about the camp commandant?"

Moss pulled him forward. "We caught him in the process of changing into prisoner's clothes. Thought he could pull a fast one on us."

"He speak English?" John asked.

Moss shrugged. "Don't think so. I slapped him around a few times and all he does is grunt."

"He does speak English," Gregory said. "He's the one who traded me for Brandon."

"What's his name?"

"Jang Yong-ho," Gregory said, struggling with the pronunciation. He pointed to one of the North Korean guards they'd rounded up. "And that guard's name is Pug Face. He's the commandant's pit bull who killed Dixon."

Moss smacked the guard across the face with the butt of his rifle.

Jang Yong-ho looked on with a blank expression.

"Where are the Americans you conscripted?" John asked the commandant, who didn't speak. John asked the man next to him. Again, no answer. "Cat got your tongue? Well, maybe you will all understand this. You're hereby charged and deemed guilty of war crimes. Care to know what your sentence is?"

Moss and the other soldiers stared at John. "Are you sure about this?" his second-in-command asked.

John pointed a finger toward the cornfield. "You walk out that gate and in two minutes you'll see a pit filled with dead Americans, all killed on this man's orders. I've never been more certain of anything in my life. Freeing ourselves from oppression will mean doing things we might not be proud of. But saving the things we love sometimes requires us to suspend the very ideals this country was founded on. Execute them now, on my order."

At once, dozens of rifles were raised up, Rough Riders as well as prisoners wielding North Korean rifles.

Jang Yong-ho and Pug Face screamed right as the men fired. John thought Gregory would look away, as he'd done many times in the past when he witnessed violent acts, but his son watched each of the men slump as they fell dead.

John drew in a long, ragged breath. "Leave them there, as a reminder of what will happen to anyone who murders innocent Americans." After that he got on the walkie and ordered his men to collect the wounded and pull back to the treeline. They were heading home.

Chapter 41

Berry Field Air National Guard Base

"When I was growing up in a small village along the banks of the Yellow River, my grandmother loved to tell the tale of Kua Fu Chasing the Sun," General Wei Liang said as he removed his hat, set it firmly on his desk and used the palm of his hand to tame a stray tuft of thinning hair. Standing before him were his four aides and all of them, including his most trusted, Colonel Guo Fenghui, wore blank expressions.

"You've not heard it?" the general asked them. He was a natural-born storyteller and might have pursued a life in the theatre had his father not pushed him to enter the military academy at a young age.

Colonel Guo shook his head.

Liang smiled. "It's an ancient and delightful tale. Long before humans, giants roamed the earth. Their leader Kua Fu was sworn to protect his people. One year the weather became incredibly hot, scorching the crops and subjecting his followers to torturous heat from the sun. Kua Fu vowed to catch the sun and bind it to his will. He chased it like the wind as it fled across the sky. As he did, the dust from his shoes became the hills and his walking stick the forests and the trees. After nine days and nights, he finally caught up to the sun, but its fire was too intense and it made him thirsty. Kua drank from the Yellow and Wei Rivers, but it wasn't enough and before he could reach the Great Lake, Kua died of thirst."

His aides continued to stare at the general, befuddled. If there was a lesson he was trying to get across, they weren't getting it.

"We owe a lot to Kua," Liang told them. "He's given us trees and land, but he had one weakness which led to his death."

"Arrogance," Guo replied.

A grin appeared on Liang's round face. "Yes. The Americans remind me in many ways of the giant Kua. They are big and powerful and capable of accomplishing many extraordinary things, except like Kua, the Americans were blinded by their own arrogance. This was why the attacks of 9/11 were so successful. Who would have thought that such a low-tech attack could be pulled off with such great effect? And wasn't the same true of our own bold attack? America's faith in her multi-layered naval and nuclear defenses led her to believe she was invulnerable to invasion. That attitude was exactly what gave China and Russia the advantage we needed. Long ago, Sun Tzu wrote, 'Pretend inferiority and encourage his arrogance.'"

Now his subordinates understood where he had been heading and many of them were nodding in agreement.

A knock came at the door and General Liang asked them to enter.

In came Colonel Li Keqiang, head of military intelligence, and the deathly paleness of his face wiped the pleasure from Liang's lips.

"What is it?"

Colonel Li handed the general a note and bowed his head.

General Liang opened the paper and read what was written. His eyes passed over the words more than once and his ears turned a slight shade of pink.

The concentration camp near Jonesboro had been overrun by a group of American insurgents. Not only had all the prisoners been released, a battalion of North Korean forces stationed nearby had nearly been wiped out when they attempted to respond. Liang kept reading and as he did his anger blossomed into a boiling rage.

"They killed the camp commandant and all of his men?" Liang asked, not entirely believing it.

Colonel Li nodded, careful not to make eye contact.

They had a handful of secret agents spread throughout what remained of the American-held territories, and none of them had warned that this sort of operation was underway. One by one the Americans had been unmasking the Chinese operatives in the field, making the collection of information more difficult. It also increased the importance of the few who remained.

"Any word from Phoenix?"

"None," Li said. "Our last report was about the attack on the truck depot near Jonesboro. The information was passed along to the commanding officer in the region." Li checked his notes. "A North Korean colonel named Chung Eui-Sun."

"The same Chung whose forces were just beaten by a group of resistance fighters?"

Li nodded. "Yes. Apparently he dismissed the threat."

"We were kind to bring our North Korean allies into the fold and yet since the beginning they've done nothing but disappoint us."

The room grew quiet. One of General Liang's four aides was a North Korean major from Pyongyang and, judging by the stoic expression he now wore, he knew better than to openly show offence at the general's comments.

"The Russians have also heard about the attack and are asking if we need their assistance."

"Absolutely not," Liang shouted back in a rare loss of control. "I'm very familiar with Russia's offers to help.

Next thing we know Federation troops will be swarming over land conquered with Chinese blood and sweat. Inform them that we're fine and that we'll handle this on our own."

"Very well, sir," Li replied.

"Who's our top special forces commander in the region?" Liang asked.

"Uh…" Li stammered, shuffling through an armful of beige folders.

"That would be Zhang Shuhong," his aide Colonel Guo said, flicking through his papers and holding one up. "I believe he and his men are currently in Houston quelling an uprising there. Before the war Zhang distinguished himself in Tibet, subduing the local population. His methods are harsh, but effective."

General Liang squared his hat back on his head and stood. "Bring me Zhang and his men by tomorrow at the latest."

Colonel Li swallowed hard. "Our radio communications are only slowly coming back up after the American EMP, but I will send a messenger by motorbike to retrieve him."

"Use smoke signals if you must," General Liang barked. "But I want him here as soon as possible and a briefing on my desk by 0600 hours with intelligence on who was behind these attacks. And do what you can about re-establishing contact with our agent in Oneida. If anyone can tell us who these people are, it'll be Phoenix."

Chapter 42

Phoenix was also the name Diane heard as she entered the mayor's office. General Brooks was with Rodriguez in the radio room, speaking with General Dempsey.

"One of my men apprehended him, General," Brooks was saying. "Saw a man acting suspiciously in the woods and went to investigate. They're on patrol for this very eventuality. We've been on high alert since our Chinese POW managed to escape."

Diane slowed down as she neared the doorway.

"Very good, General Brooks. You've proven yourself a terrific asset to the cause. Have your people managed to extract any information from the suspect?"

"Nothing useful yet, sir," Brooks replied, "but I assure you my men are using every means at their disposal to pull what we can from the Chinese agent."

"Our boys intercepted a coded Chinese radio message about an attack on the prison camp outside Jonesboro. Seems like not all of their equipment was fried."

"That happens, sir," Brooks replied. "Even an EMP can't bat a thousand."

"Yes, but Colonel Mack and his men have not yet returned."

Diane's spine stiffened. Could freeing Jonesboro have been the mission John left on? The idea was tantalizing. It meant she might soon be hugging Brandon and her son, right before she admonished them both for having run off in the first place.

"I like his initiative," Dempsey said. "I only wish we had more officers like him."

"Colonel Mack isn't a regular officer," Brooks said.

"What do you mean? He isn't a colonel?"

"He's a retired Iraq vet who's also the acting mayor of Oneida," Brooks told him. "Was a lieutenant with the 278th ACR, if I remember correctly. I reactivated him and boosted his rank to colonel when we arrived so he could issue orders."

"Great thinking, General. Looks like you picked a winner."

Even from the hallway, Diane could feel the blood boiling in Brooks' veins. She walked by then, and waved at the general as she passed, the tiniest hint of a smirk on her lips.

•••

Diane found Emma out back, feeding George handfuls of wild grass.

"I think he's sad," Emma said, petting the bird's head with one hand, the other cupping under its beak.

Diane laughed. "What makes you say that?"

"I think he needs a girlfriend."

George paced around his tiny enclosure, waiting for Emma to hand him more grass.

"You think he's lonely?" Diane asked.

"Sure. How many geese do you see in this town?"

"You do have a point there." Diane paused and studied her daughter's hands. They were trembling. "What do you suggest?"

"Maybe when Gregory and Brandon get back we can head to Stanley Lake and see if we can find a girlfriend for George. I don't want him to grow old never knowing what it's like to have someone to love."

Diane curled an arm around Emma. "I hope you haven't given up on finding Brandon and your brother."

Emma tossed a few blades of grass into the enclosure and watched them drop to the ground in spirals. "I hope he got the message I sent him in the leaflet."

"I'm sure he did," Diane said reassuringly.

Emma smiled. "You know, sometimes I look at George in his enclosure and it makes me think of Gregory."

"You mean because they're both prisoners?"

"Not really. Remember when Gregory was four and he got that bone infection—"

"Osteomyelitis," Diane said, puzzled. "Yes, I remember vividly. Your brother was an active little boy who fell on his knees one too many times. Doctor said the infection must have entered through the broken skin on his kneecaps, got into his blood and then the bone around his knee. They threaded a PICC line through the vein in his upper arm to his heart in order to drip-feed him his antibiotics."

"I was only six," Emma said, "but I still remember how he used to bounce around in his playpen, frustrated that he couldn't get out and go play."

Diane felt the tears coming and fought hard to keep them at bay. Her eyes found George again, waddling back and forth within the confines of his cage. "I guess I see what you mean."

"He came home on Christmas Day," Emma said. "I remember that most of all because I thought it was the best present I ever got."

Diane pulled her daughter in tight.

Looking up at her, Emma grew serious. "And don't you ever tell him what I just said."

Now Diane did laugh. "Your brother knows you love him, Emma. Even if you're too proud to tell him yourself."

Chapter 43

John and his Rough Riders returned to Oneida exhausted from the long and dangerous journey home. When they emerged from the woods and onto Alberta Street, many of the workers busy repairing buildings or bolstering the town's defenses stopped what they were doing to marvel at the sight.

The men on horseback rode with one and sometimes two children seated behind them. Others had adults too frail or sick to walk. In all, John had returned with over a hundred former POWs, the rest having scattered in all directions to form resistance groups of their own. At least that was the hope.

Seated behind John was his son Gregory, who hadn't dared let go since they'd set off from Jonesboro. It was only when Diane pulled up in a golf cart, her face a mask of disbelief and joy, that Gregory slipped off and ran to her. The rest of the column returned to the stables. John told Moss he wouldn't be long.

The streets were noticeably fuller now that parts of the 3rd Infantry Division had showed up. The stress it put on food management was no doubt high, but with rationing of resources, John was sure they would be fine. As long as everyone pulled their own weight.

After dismounting, John went to the crowd gathering around Gregory and Diane.

"You take off like that again and I'll kill you myself," Diane said, squeezing him.

Gregory tried to smile, but it was clear he was weak

and needed rest and maybe something warm to eat.

"Where did you find him?" a man with a sledgehammer asked.

The mission had been kept a tight secret and John was happy to see it had stayed that way. But now that they were back he saw no reason to maintain the subterfuge. He told the citizens assembled how they'd attacked and freed a camp with American prisoners.

Ray Gruber came out of the crowd to congratulate John. "I'm just glad you made it back in one piece," he said, patting his friend on the shoulder and beaming that contagious smile of his.

Surely there was a joke coming John's way, but not everyone had made it home. They'd suffered casualties and there was nothing funny about that.

"A lot's happened since you've been away," Ray told him.

Diane kissed the top of Gregory's head and looked up. "We caught Phoenix," she said.

"Stop being humble, Diane. If it wasn't for you spotting him in the woods, he woulda slipped through the cracks for sure. He's being interrogated by General Brooks' men as we speak."

Now it was John's turn to show surprise. "Who was it?"

"David Newbury," Ray said. "An American born and bred. Can you believe it? The guy pretends to have escaped from a concentration camp and sets out to betray Oneida and its people. Who knows how many have died because of him."

This wasn't at all what John had expected. The news was terrific, of course, and it certainly made sense that the Chinese might have managed to pressure David into working for them. Hopefully, John would get his chance to ask the man a few questions.

"I'll let General Brooks know you're back," Ray said.

"I'm sure he'll want a debriefing as soon as possible."

"Not yet, Ray," John said. "First, I want some time with my family."

"Understood," Ray said, smiling. "Whenever you're ready."

•••

John found a quiet spot near the greenhouses where he could sit and talk with his family. A few minutes later, Diane returned with Emma, who'd been at the newspaper office preparing another batch of leaflets.

"You know you coulda gotten yourself killed," Emma started in as she climbed out of the golf cart.

"It's not your place to discipline your brother," John told her. "This is the first time we've been together in a while. There'll be plenty of time for choice words later."

Gregory's eyes fell to the grass at his feet. He was still wearing his prison uniform.

"I swung by the house and brought you some fresh clothes," Diane said. "Why don't you scoot behind the shed over there and get out of those rags."

Gregory took the clothes and left.

"What about Brandon?" Emma asked. "Is he with the others at the stable?"

John glanced back at his horse who was a few feet away, nibbling on grass. "Yeah, that's something we need to talk to you about."

The muscles in Emma's face tensed. "If something happened I don't wanna hear about it." She pushed her fingers into her ears.

"Come on, honey," Diane said, gently easing her arms down. She turned to John. "Where is he?"

John conveyed Gregory's story about Brandon being conscripted into the Chinese army.

Emma stood in disbelief. "How's that even possible?

I mean, why doesn't he just run away?"

"It's really not that simple," John tried to explain. "Brandon believes if he breaks his word then Gregory might be killed."

"Yes, but Gregory's here with us now." Tears filled Emma's eyes and John understood perfectly well. A big part of her drive to make those leaflets had come from her desire to be reunited with Brandon.

"He and the others were taken away before we arrived. But I've got people out searching for him."

Emma's face sank into her hands as she began to sob. Gregory returned just then, a greasy-haired kid with a dirty face dressed in fresh jeans and t-shirt.

"What's wrong with her?" he asked.

"Don't ask," John said. "Right now, we're just so thrilled to have you back."

Gregory nodded and tried to smile, but John could see there was an ocean of pain behind those eyes. The kind of suffering a child should never have to experience. There was no telling what sort of atrocities he'd witnessed in that camp. Only the mass grave they'd found nearby and the hollow look in his son's eyes hinted at the damage that had already been done.

But in many ways, John's own experiences with PTSD had made him intimately familiar with the tortured corridors of a traumatized mind and soul. The pain hadn't killed him, although it had certainly come close. And while Gregory might have been physically freed from the camps, John knew he might never be free from the memories of what went on there.

Chapter 44

The debriefing room at the mayor's office was stifling hot and John undid the top button of his fatigues to cool off. A fan would have been nice, but the town's limited power supply was dedicated for construction and infrastructure work.

Seated at the conference table next to him were Moss, Ray Gruber, Henry, General Brooks and Colonel Higgs. John went over the details of the mission to free the camp.

"How will we keep in touch with these disparate fighting groups you've sent off?" Higgs asked. "Is there any way to coordinate them?"

John motioned to the radio operator. "This is where Henry comes in. As far as I understand it, he's begun a daily radio broadcast for members of the resistance. Think BBC during World War II."

"Without the funny accent," Ray chimed in.

"We should be able to relay target information to them in code through Henry's daily broadcasts. The trick will be letting the insurgents in on the code itself."

Higgs seemed pleased.

"Henry's already got something of a following all over the country," John said. "And not only in the occupied zone. Didn't one woman ask you to marry her?"

The room erupted into laughter.

"Just don't let it go to your head, pretty boy," Moss said, punching him lightly in the shoulder. "I heard she asked Rodriguez first, but he turned her down."

When the joviality died down, General Brooks reached into a wooden crate at his feet and set a crude-looking mortar round on the table. A series of white wires snaked out from the nose like strands of cooked spaghetti.

"Something tells me this ain't your father's mortar," Moss said, leaning back in his chair and flicking a hand through the bristling hairs of his mohawk.

"We gave it some thought and realized that our fledgling armaments factory needed to narrow its production line to a single item," General Brooks explained. "And this is it."

"A mortar round that can double as an IED," John said.

Brooks patted it as though it were a newborn puppy. "Sure, it looks crude, but this baby is packed with enough explosives to knock out a tank."

Everyone in the room looked uneasy.

"Don't worry, folks," the general reassured them. "This one's only a demo. But I've got nearly three dozen townspeople trained in how to make them. In a week from now I'll have double that number."

"My team that's planting IEDs along I-40 could really use these," John said. "They've been keeping a low profile over the last few days, but they're very skilled at living off the land and doing what they can to disrupt those Chinese supply lines."

General Brooks grinned. "And with Phoenix taken care of, we can reduce the need for so much secrecy around here."

"Have you gotten anything useful out of him?" John asked.

General Brooks shook his head. "No, but not for lack of trying. He claims he'd gone into the woods to go to the bathroom and not hand over secrets to the enemy."

"Hey, at least his excuse is original," Moss said, grinning.

"I wouldn't mind having a word with him," John suggested.

General Brooks didn't seem to like that idea. "You can when we're done."

"Frankly, I think he should be taken out back and shot," Ray said. "Just think how much American blood is on his hands."

John knew this wasn't a time for rash emotional decisions. Brooks was right to work the spy and perhaps if they were lucky, they might even be able to convince him to swap sides.

Moss slapped the table hard. "You know, I still can't believe that David Newbury sold us out. His intel on the camp was really accurate."

"That is true," John told them. "I also have to say our attack took the North Koreans completely by surprise."

"And I believe there's a very good reason for that," General Brooks replied, removing the demo IED and placing it back in the box at his feet. "We've come to understand that there are rifts between the members of the Eastern Alliance. The Chinese hold the North Koreans in contempt and the Russians feel the same way about both of their Asian allies."

"There might be an opportunity to exploit that," John said, rubbing the three-day-old stubble on his chin. Neither he nor Moss had shaved in days.

"With the attack on the concentration camp, I believe you already have," Brooks replied. "The goal now is to push that even further."

"If we can get our hands on some Chinese army uniforms," Moss said, "and attack a North Korean outpost, then we may be able to do just that."

"I'll bring some members of the 3rd Infantry Division into the Rough Riders and put them in charge of that," John said. As much as he would like to, he couldn't be part of every single operation they launched. He would need to delegate command to subgroups of operatives, as he'd done with the IED team.

Ray cleared his throat, still pink around the neck from his impassioned plea for Phoenix's execution. "If you're looking for a juicy target, I may have picked up something of interest."

Ripples appeared on General Brooks' brow. "What's your source?"

"I got a little shortwave in the shed behind my house. One I was using back when Oneida was trying to warn other communities about the danger of fifth columnists like The Chairman. Even built my own Faraday cage and everything." Ray glanced up and saw the impatience on the faces around him. "Anyway, one of the contacts I made near Los Angeles harbor told me yesterday he saw a large supply shipment being sent east by rail. Must be at least a dozen trains loaded with armor and fuel set to run through the Midwest all the way to Knoxville. I should be able to find out what line they're on. Some of those IEDs you're making might come in handy." Ray grinned widely, exposing the fillings in his back molars.

John and the others were impressed.

"And here I was convinced you were an aspiring stand-up comedian," Moss quipped.

Ray let out a hearty laugh. "I'll take that as a compliment."

"Sounds promising," Brooks said and turned to John. "I want you to put together a plan as soon as possible."

John nodded and made a note.

The general motioned to Higgs. The colonel went to

the door and made sure it was closed. "Before we wrap this meeting up," Brooks said, "I want to share some news I recently learned from General Dempsey. Our 3rd and 7th Fleets in the Pacific were not destroyed by the enemy as we originally feared. When the EMP struck, they were both docked in Australian ports, where they stayed for several months, unable to make contact with home. Apparently returns from Alice Springs' over-the-horizon radar indicated a massive surge of activity along the eastern coast of China. The CIA and NSA agents in Pine Springs at the time were quick to reach out to the governments of Australia and New Zealand on behalf of the United States, suspecting correctly that our capital and the country's nerve center had been destroyed. Retrofitting the ships to use GLONASS satellite navigation gave our men the eyes they needed to begin planning a counterattack. From there the joint navies of America, Australia and New Zealand set out to retake the Pacific and cut off the Eastern Alliance's lines of supply from the sea."

"Heck, it's about time," Moss said excitedly.

"All we know so far is that we've had some small victories and suffered losses. The battles in the Pacific continue to rage at this very moment and as I get more information, I'll be sure to pass it along."

Henry put his hand up. "Can I include this in my daily broadcast for *The Voice of Freedom*?"

"I was hoping you would," Brooks replied with enthusiasm. "But what I'm about to tell you gentlemen next can't leave this room. Last night at approximately 0600 hours, a large NATO force landed near Halifax and took the port, opening a new front to the north. As the reinforcements from our European allies begin to flow, it should relieve some of the pressure on our boys along the Appalachians. It still isn't clear whether that NATO force will move west against the Russians or south to threaten the Chinese left flank."

Either way it didn't matter. America was no longer standing alone and the cheers that went up were so loud and spontaneous, General Brooks struggled to quiet them down. "It's important we keep this under wraps for now," he told them. "The Chinese are struggling to get their communications and supply lines back up and running. We'd hate to leak news of a surprise attack and ruin the whole thing."

Chapter 45

General Wei Liang peered down from the VIP box at the fighting spectacle organized for the entertainment of his men. The improvised ring and stands, finished late last night, now contained nearly ten thousand PLA soldiers, enjoying some time away from the front lines. In the ring was a top kung-fu martial artist flown in from Hong Kong. Against him was an American POW Liang had had shipped up from one of the camps in Alabama. The American was bigger, of course, but what the Asian fighter lacked in strength, he more than made up for in speed and technique. Regardless, this would be an interesting battle and one that would help to feed Liang's itch for gambling. The Chinese fighter was favored six to one and so Liang had discreetly put twenty-five thousand yuan on the American.

The bell had no sooner sounded than the kung-fu fighter charged out, swinging his fists and kicking aggressively. The bulky American backed away, his arms working to block the furious assault.

Just then an unusually tall, handsome Chinese soldier approached the general.

"You asked to see me?" he said, passing Liang's guards and entering the VIP booth.

Down in the ring, the kung-fu fighter ducked a wild punch from the American and countered with a hammerblow strike to the chest. The crowd went wild.

"Your reputation for quelling anti-Communist uprisings in Tibet precedes you," General Liang said without averting his eyes from the spectacle. The man next to him was Zhang Shuhong. Six foot two, with chiseled features, he was a special forces commander who, like the general, had come from a humble background in the city of Xinyu, southern China.

"I take pride in my work, sir."

Confident, but not too cocky. Any more and he would have suspected Zhang was trying to compensate for some hidden insecurity.

Both men watched the fight for a moment in silence. The American wasn't doing very well and the crowd was loving every minute of it.

"I asked you here to fix a problem for me."

"Yes, I heard of the attack on Camp Shènglì." The word meant 'victory.' The irony wasn't lost on either man.

Since the incident, two more camps had been brazenly overrun by American insurgents. Now even more prisoners were on the loose and the escalating problem was beginning to eat up resources Liang couldn't spare. He'd asked Zhang here to help him stem the bleeding. He handed the commander a folder.

Zhang opened it, reading the first of a series of dossiers. "John Mack. Age forty-five. A retired lieutenant with the 278th Armored Cavalry Regiment."

"That should read colonel," Liang said. "He's been promoted."

"What are the Rough Riders?" Zhang asked, scanning the page.

"Apparently it's the name they've given their particular insurgency group."

Zhang smiled. "Sounds like something from a western."

Returning the gesture, the general said, "I assumed

the same thing. They're in love with that bygone era and fail to see the future even when it's staring them in the face. I want him and his men caught. Dead or alive. Either one is acceptable. And when you're done, Mack's corpse will be displayed as a warning to anyone who dares stand against us."

Down in the ring, the kung-fu fighter threw a spinning back kick. The move was caught by the American, who swept his legs out from under him. The larger man then fell on top of his small, but agile foe, slowly working him into a choke hold.

The sound of the Asian man's neck snapping stunned the crowd into silence. Their surprise was so complete that the smirk on Liang's face went unnoticed by those around him. It was the look of a man who was heading for a winning streak.

Chapter 46

The light from an oil lamp flickered off the walls of the Rough Rider headquarters. In the planning room, John, Moss and Specialist Heller, the explosives expert from Alpha squad, were pouring over maps of Lenoir City, Tennessee, an area south of Oak Ridge and west of Knoxville. A section of the Norfolk Southern Railway line ran through the town, hugging the Little Tennessee River on its way to Knoxville. John followed it with his finger until he came to a turn in the rail line.

"This is where we'll set the IEDs," he told them.

"On a curve?" Moss asked, moving closer to get a better look at the map.

"Always," John told him. "First off, it'll give us the best chance of derailing the train."

Heller's eyes lit up. "And second, there are plenty more straight tracks than curved ones so repair will be more difficult."

"Precisely. We'll wire up three mortars buried beneath the tracks and attached to a pressure plate. As soon as the Chinese steam engine rolls over it, the IEDs will blow and derail the train along with its supply cars." John glanced over his notes. "Only six of us will be going on this one."

"What about the others?" Moss asked.

"I've got another Rough Rider team under Hoffman heading east toward Johnson City to take out a low-level Chinese general. Another group is going west to attack a North Korean checkpoint dressed as Chinese soldiers."

"You found the uniforms?" Moss asked.

John shook his head. "Sort of. We decided to use what we pulled off the dead Chinese soldiers who attacked the town. It took a bit of mix-and-matching, but I think it turned out all right."

Heller didn't look convinced. "Don't you think they'll be able to tell Americans from their own people?"

"No one at the checkpoint will be left alive to talk about it, but we've picked a place where there'll be plenty of witnesses. From a distance, all they'll see are Chinese uniforms."

Nodding, Moss said, "You want the North Koreans to think the Chinese are giving them payback for failing to stop the attack on the truck depot and the concentration camp."

"Bingo. Listen, they may not totally buy it, but I wanna plant a seed of doubt in their minds. Anything we can do to drive a wedge into this fragile alliance only works in our favor."

A knock came at the door and John pulled it open to find Gregory. He checked his watch, seeing that it was nearly eleven at night. "I thought you were asleep?"

"I tried. Kept tossing and turning."

John glanced back at Moss and Heller. "I'm kinda in the middle of something important, bud. There's a couch over there. Why don't you lie down and try to get some rest."

Gregory did and John couldn't help but wonder if the horrifying images of what he'd seen at the camp were keeping his son from sleeping.

As the meeting resumed, the look of unabashed optimism on Moss' face was almost contagious. "You know me, boss, I'm about as skeptical as they come, but I'm starting to feel like we may have a real chance of winning this thing."

John nodded, but didn't say anything.

"I mean, that meeting we had with General Brooks. Australia and New Zealand helping us in the Pacific. The NATO landings. We aren't alone anymore."

John let out a sigh as he rearranged the papers on the desk.

"What is it?"

"Heller, will you excuse us for a moment?" John said.

"Sure thing," the specialist replied, confused. "I'll start putting those pressure plates together."

When he left the room, Moss took a step back, his body stiffening as though John were about to lay into him.

"There's something you need to know about that meeting with Brooks," John said.

"I don't like that look on your face."

"The intel on the war in the Pacific is accurate, but that NATO force..." John trailed off.

"What are you saying?" Moss asked. It looked like he'd just been kicked in the gut.

"I'm saying I've heard from other sources the landing in Halifax isn't nearly what Brooks made it out to be. It's far closer to the Dieppe raid than it is to D-Day. We know and trust each other, which is why I'm telling you this. I just didn't want you getting your hopes too high."

"But why feed us a bunch of lies?" Moss said, baring his teeth. "And don't feed me a line about morale and propaganda."

"It is, in part," John admitted. "It's also about making sure everyone's on the same team."

"But we caught Phoenix," Moss almost pleaded and then paused. "You mean there might be more spies?"

"I don't think so," John said. "But Brooks is just making sure."

Another knock at the door and this time Moss was the one who answered it.

Henry looked up at them, his shoulders drooping. "I've got some bad news."

"There's a shocker," Moss spat.

"We've just got some intel that the team you sent to plant IEDs along I-40 have been killed."

John felt the blood drain from his cheeks. "Any word how it happened?" he asked, his fingers curling into tight fists.

"We've only got one army translator, but from the bits of chatter we're picking up, it sounds like they were taken out by Chinese special forces."

John tapped an index finger on the map table. "Okay, Henry. Thank you." His radio operator turned to leave when John called him back. "Keep this between us for now, will you? I wouldn't want this sort of news getting out."

A hint of reluctance showed on Henry's face before he acknowledged the order and closed the door behind him.

"It was only a question of time," John told his number two, "before they brought in counter-insurgency teams."

"Those are the risks," Moss replied. "But do you really think keeping it a secret is the best play? We've already got a handful of top people thinking the cavalry's on its way from Halifax harbor to help turn things in our favor. Have we become a nation of folks who lie for the greater good? I mean, the EMP was a horrible thing to happen, but it's given us another shot at starting over. At doing it right this time."

"America didn't invent state secrets, Moss. As much as the world likes to blame us for everything that goes wrong around the globe, this game's been going on for thousands of years. Revolutions have been fought over the centuries to overthrow elements of human nature we can't change. The Russians tried in vain to end inequality by ushering in a system that failed to take into account the realities of what makes us tick. Whether we like it or not, each of us is controlled by our emotions. Before the EMP a huge chunk of the population voted for new presidents based on how they looked and a few choice soundbites. If he'd been born decades later, a wheelchair-bound president like Franklin D. Roosevelt would have faced a resounding defeat. So you're right. We do have a chance to change things, but we can't change the wiring deep down. People need hope and sometimes you need to keep that flame from going out by withholding the bad news and exaggerating the good." John grew quiet for a moment before he said, "I wish I could say more, but you'll understand soon enough."

Chapter 47

When Diane awoke the next morning, John had already left. Another mission and another roll of the dice, she thought philosophically. He'd come home late the night before, carrying a sleeping Gregory in his arms, as well as a look of remorse. That normally meant some bad news had arrived, something connected to an order he'd given in the past. Diane could read it in her husband's body language, the way his spine seemed slightly bent under a tremendous weight.

After a quick breakfast with the kids, she headed to the greenhouse. If all went well, it would finally be back in operation. Already, with the recent influx of soldiers from the 3rd Infantry Division, the strain on their resources had grown significantly. The power from Ray Gruber's two windmills was going to be a huge help, running the lights, power tools and the hydroponic greenhouse. And that was one of the reasons why the sight that greeted her at the greenhouse was so disturbing.

The blades on one of the windmills had stopped turning. Two men on Diane's team were doing their best to figure out how to fix it, but she knew this was no place to be poking around. They needed Ray.

She asked around and no one had seen him yet this morning. The vice mayor wasn't normally one to oversleep and so Diane set off to find him, doing her best to ignore the nagging concern wiggling its way through her belly.

She weaved her golf cart through Oneida's zigzagging back streets. In several places the rubble and burned-out hulks of Chinese military vehicles had been left in place to tie up any armored assault launched by the enemy. In others, small paths had been opened about the width of a golf cart to allow thin lines of traffic to pass. But the inconvenience did more than threaten to tie up a fresh batch of Chinese invaders. The mornings and evenings saw long lines of congestion Diane had thought they'd left behind them.

Rodriguez was on his way to the radio room when she drove past him. She pulled to a stop and asked if he'd seen Ray, explaining why it was important. She didn't go so far as to say she was worried something had happened to him. Ray's knowledge of wind power and AC/DC power conversion made him a prime target for any Chinese agent they might have missed. Not that she needed to spell things out to someone as intelligent as Rodriguez.

With that, Rodriguez hopped on board and they sped toward the house Ray was staying in, a bungalow a short ways off Alberta Street. They arrived and knocked several times only to find the house empty.

"I'm sure he's somewhere around town," Rodriguez said, perhaps trying to placate Diane's overactive imagination. "He's probably at the mayor's office, giving General Brooks an earful of bad jokes."

"I came from there on my way to the greenhouses and I didn't see him anywhere around."

Rodriguez sighed as the two made their way around the house into the backyard. Like many of the homes in town, the grass had been left to grow to nearly two feet high. Diane went to the sliding glass door and squished her face up to the cold surface, cutting the glare with a cupped hand. She scanned around inside without finding anything out of place.

"You hear that?" Rodriguez asked.

She did and it sounded like static and mumbled voices. It took a few seconds to figure out that it was coming from the brown shed in the corner of Ray's backyard.

They approached and slowed as they drew closer. The voices coming from inside got louder, clearer.

"Please confirm you received my last transmission, over."

It was Ray all right and Diane couldn't help wondering who he was talking to. Most of the communication from Oneida was being performed by Henry or Rodriguez from the radio room in the mayor's office.

But the next thing she heard from inside the shed took Diane's breath away.

"Red Dragon, this is Phoenix, please come in."

Chapter 48

It was nearly 1800 hours by the time John and the five men who had joined him on this mission reached the outskirts of Lenoir City on horseback. Accompanying him were Moss, Devon, Reese, Heller and Gardner, Bravo's squad leader. They'd been in the saddle since the early dawn hours, skirting enemy checkpoints and troops concentrations. Heller and Gardner would prep and plant the IEDs on the train tracks while John, Devon and Moss provided security. Reese was their insurance policy. A water tower on the edge of town would provide him with a clear field of fire over the entire area of operation.

After the sniper split off from them, John made one final radio check to ensure their communications were still operational.

"You're our eyes out here, Reese. Call out any approaching threats. This may be our only shot at stopping that supply train and any others coming up behind it."

"I'm on it, Colonel," the sniper said, huffing as he used a Dumpster to climb onto the roof of a nearby store. The thirty-pound Barrett .50 caliber rifle he'd brought for the job could cut a man in two, although this was the kind of mission where having to use it meant you'd already failed.

Before long, John and the others came to the sharp

turn in the track. He pointed to an area five meters before the curve. "This is where I want you to plant those IEDs," he told Heller and Gardner. They led the horses into the forest nearby and tied them securely to several trees. With care, they removed the improvised explosive mortar rounds, the pressure plates, two spades and a sledgehammer. The latter was what the two men would use to pop the spikes and position the bombs; the work would be loud for a moment or two, but hopefully not enough to draw any unwanted attention.

John and Devon positioned themselves along the southern treeline while Devon found a clump of bushes north of the tracks. Once security was in place, Heller and Gardner got in place and went to work. Two loud whacks with the sledgehammer made John wince.

"How's the coast?" he asked Reese over the radio.

"Still clear. Wait a minute."

John's heart froze in his chest. He signaled for Gardner and Heller to stop and drop down. "What do you see?"

"Hmm, maybe nothing. I got a group of women about two hundred yards west of your position. Looks like they're carrying buckets of water up from the river."

"River water near a big city," Moss said. "I guess that's one way to kill yourself." He leaned into John's walkie. "Do they look hot?"

Reese snickered. "Negative. Unless you're into women who look like men. Either way, they're gone now, so tell Moss if he wants a shot at them he'll need to give chase."

"All right," John said, giving the two on the tracks the all-clear. "Maintain radio silence unless you see something."

Gardner and Heller were digging gravel out from under one of the rails when a series of shots rang out.

Rounds thudded into the ground around Heller and Gardner, dinging off the gravel and the railroad tracks. Then came what sounded like a stick smacking a wet rag as a bullet struck Gardner in the temple. Blood and bone sprayed Heller, who was kneeling beside him.

"Get back," John yelled as he depressed the actuator on his walkie. "Reese, we're coming under fire. We have a man down and no visual on the enemy."

Heller's chest exploded in a red mist as he turned to flee. Blood dribbled from his lips as he slumped over the train tracks. Now Devon was opening up to the west, presumably the direction from which they'd been fired on, but the truth was, in the chaos it was hard to tell what was coming from where.

Moss jumped up and charged out to grab hold of Heller. John edged out from the wood line and peered through his scope. A group of men in black fatigues were hugging the wall of a nearby building as they moved toward them.

"Reese," John called out over the walkie. "I've got three tangos on your three o'clock, red-brick building. South side."

Reese didn't answer, but his Barrett did. The distinctive boom of his sniper rifle sounded just as John was laying down his own covering fire. The .50 cal round impacted the first two men, who were standing in a line, painting their insides against the wall next to them. The third soldier ran for cover. A second blast from Reese's Barrett killed the third man. Although the sniper's fire was helping to suppress the enemy, the deafening percussion was threatening to give away his position.

Moss pulled Heller back to the tree line as more fire came in, this time from the east.

"They're all around us," Moss gasped, checking for signs of life.

"What about Gardner?"

"He's gone. Took a direct hit to the head. Didn't feel a thing."

John called out to Devon to cover the east.

"We don't get out of here soon, boss, we never will."

John nodded, scanning through his ACOG for the source of the fire they were taking.

"Colonel," Reese said, "I'm taking fire from somewhere west of you. My position's been compromised."

"Don't wait for us, Reese. Soon as you're off that roof, hightail it back to Oneida. We'll meet you there."

"Affirmative," the sniper said, the sound of rounds pinging off the metal siding before him nearly drowning out his words.

"We're gonna need to make a break for it," John told Moss. "You grab the horses while Devon and I lay down some covering fire." He turned to tell Devon to cover the western approach when a round went straight through the young soldier's neck. Devon's eyes grew impossibly wide as he dropped his weapon and clamped his hands down over the wound. The next shot was fatal and Devon fell face forward into the brush.

The human part of John wanted to scream. The blond young man had started as a member of Moss' security team and had become something of a surrogate son to John. Staggering back on legs weakened with disbelief, John untied his horse and grabbed the reins of another. They would need to leave one horse behind. He and Moss charged out from the forest's edge, without any covering fire. The rounds came as soon as they hit the train tracks. The brown mare John was holding with his right hand took a hit, whinnied and dropped. Bullets seemed to be coming in from every direction as he and Moss leapt over the tracks and into the woods beyond. For a moment the firing stopped as the gunmen gave chase.

With three of his best men lying dead and their own fate yet to be decided, one thing was clear. This hadn't been a case of bad luck. Someone had been waiting for them.

Chapter 49

Knoxville, one hundred and sixty days before EMP

"You mentioned looking for a job, John," Tom Bukowski, his VA counselor, said. "How's that going?"

John removed his 278th Armored Cavalry ball cap and rested it on one knee. "Pretty good, I'd say. I've always been pretty handy, so I guess it seemed natural to start a small general contracting business."

"That's great. And what about the drinking?"

Nodding, John rubbed his lips with the tips of his fingers. "Some days are better than others. I haven't touched a drop in weeks. But I don't think alcoholism was ever my problem."

"Really?"

"Drinking was an easy way of numbing the pain. Could as easily have been oxycodone if I'd been more seriously wounded, like some of the men I served with."

Tom nodded and smiled.

Nearly seven months before, after Diane had confronted him about his drinking, John had taken her advice and paid a visit to his local Veterans' Counseling Center. He'd explained that he was having trouble readjusting to civilian life. After a short wait, they'd introduced him to one of the counselors: Tom Bukowski, a former Army intelligence officer who'd been deployed to the Former Yugoslav Republic of Macedonia and Bosnia as well as North Africa. He was round-headed and quick to smile. John had taken to the man. They'd even served in some of the same theatres of operation, which had helped to put his mind at ease.

John's greatest reservation about getting help had been being labelled a coward and letting down the men he'd served with. Although he had known on some level that something inside wasn't right, he'd never had a name for it. He hadn't spent more than a few minutes describing the feelings plaguing him before Tom had suggested he might be suffering from post-traumatic stress disorder. During the Civil War it was known as the soldier's heart; in World War I, shell shock; and in World War II, battle fatigue. Differing names aside, the symptoms had largely been the same. Lack of sleep, loss of concentration, increased irritability, drinking and drug use and in some cases violence or suicide.

The explanation had made him think immediately of his former JTAC Christopher Lewis. Had his friend gone to seek help? John doubted it. If he had, he would likely be alive today. Struggling, as most frontline combat veterans were, but alive nonetheless.

The two men sat on soft folding chairs facing each other in one of the session rooms when they spoke. It was meant to be relaxed and informal.

"You know how important it is to stay active," Tom told him, clicking the end of his pen. "In the months we've been meeting, you've opened up about the guilt you carry around over the death of men under you. That feeling might never go away completely, but it's important, at least for now, that you keep pouring your energy into something positive."

John reached behind and produced a white plastic tube. He unplugged one end and removed a rolled-up piece of paper. "Funny you should mention that. I've been sketching out some plans I'd like you to have a look at." John handed the rolled paper over and Tom opened it, studying the image.

"What is this?" Tom asked.

"It's my pod."

"Your what?"

"I've got some money set aside and decided to take your advice about funneling my energy into more constructive pursuits. You've been around the world, so I don't need to tell you we live in a country that's been largely sheltered from civil unrest. Everything we have is built on a precarious foundation that could come crashing down if the economy goes belly up or the lights are ever shut off for good."

"You're talking about an apocalyptic scenario," Tom said, looking uncomfortable.

"Call it what you want," John replied. "I'm not one of those guys standing on street corners with drool down my chin prophesising the end of the world or anything. But if I learned anything in the military it was that redundancy is key. You know how they say, 'No plan survives first contact?' Well, through our sessions I've come to understand why I've had such a difficult time readjusting. I'd adapted."

Tom looked at him quizzically. "Adapted? In what way?"

"I'd adapted to an environment in Iraq where threats were constant and unpredictable. There was no safe hiding place and that had me always on edge. And once the threat had dissipated, I found it was impossible to turn that survival mode off. It was a winning state of mind in Iraq, but a losing one back home." John rubbed the scar that ran across the palm of his hand. "The pimply kid packing your groceries probably isn't a threat, neither is your son's grade-school teacher, but when you apply the mindset which saved your behind in Iraq to the folks back home, you start looking crazy."

Tom looked pensive. "So you feel that channeling those feelings into helping to protect your family in a worst-case scenario has helped?"

"No question," John replied. "The trick is to not become paranoid about it. Could be that after it's built I never need that pod or the cabin we have up north, but I'd rather be prepared than worried about how I might look to my neighbors."

"And what about the nightmares?" Tom asked. "Have they begun to fade?"

John shook his head, staring at the ground. "No. Those will always be a part of me, I know that now. Sometimes when the pressure gets to be too much, I still wake up in a cold sweat. I guess there's some part of me that still wishes I could go back and change things. I've made mistakes, I won't lie, and at some point I'll have to answer for what I did. That I can live with, Doc, but the hardest part will be answering for what I failed to do."

Chapter 50

Oneida. Present.

Returning to town, John felt like he'd reached a new low. The mission had been one of his worst personal failures of the war. Heller, Gardner and Devon, three top-notch men, were dead and it was beginning to look like they'd been sent headfirst into an ambush.

The entire trek home, none of the men had said a word. Each was wrapped up in their own thoughts. What went wrong and who had tried to have them killed? For John, one person kept popping up, someone who had more likely than not never expected them to make it home to voice their suspicions.

Ray Gruber was an integral part of Oneida's administrative team and a man who'd proven himself time and time again. This entire mission was based on his suggestion, his intelligence. But suspicions weren't proof and John knew that drawing those kinds of conclusions when emotions were running high led to vigilante justice.

The streets were practically empty as they entered town. John, Moss and Reese exchanged curious looks. Up ahead, the vague outline of a crowd took shape. They seemed to be shouting.

"The heck's going on?" John asked no one in particular.

Moss unshouldered his M4 and laid it across his lap as they rode down Alberta Street. "Hard to say, boss, but angry mobs are never a good sign."

"Looks like they're gathered in front of the jail," Reese said.

The closer they got, the clearer the crowd's chant became. "Lynch him," they were shouting over and over.

"What's this all about?" John asked a man in overalls who stood stiffly, hands planted on his hips.

"Caught another one of them Chinese spies," the man told him. "And you won't guess who it is."

John bet he did, but let the man tell him anyway.

"The vice mayor," he said, jabbing an accusing finger at John. "Your right-hand man. I could understand that drifter David Newbury, but Ray Gruber?"

Dismounting, John passed the reins of his horse to Moss and pushed his way through the crowd. Not surprisingly he found the front door to the jail locked and banged three times. Rodriguez answered and John struggled to get in past the clamoring crowd.

"Can you believe those people?" Rodriguez said. "I didn't see them getting bent out of shape when David was caught."

"Maybe because to them he was a nobody," John said. "These people trusted Ray. Saw him every day. Thought he was one of them."

"Hey, how did the mission go?"

"Not now," John cut him off. "Bring me to Ray."

"He's being held in a cell with two guards. They got him on suicide watch. Your wife and I caught him sending messages to his Chinese contact."

John looked him right in the eye. "Was he using his radio?"

Rodriguez nodded.

"None of us knew he had one before that last meeting," John said. "We were all so focused on the intel coming in we didn't think anything of it."

The two men made their way upstairs to the holding cell area.

"What does this mean for Newbury?" Rodriguez asked.

"Frankly, I'm not sure. I was never a hundred percent convinced he fit the profile of a top-level Chinese spy," John said. "More importantly, he was never privy to any high-level meetings. He spent most of his time sick in the hospital with Dr. Coffee, for goodness' sake, biding his time till he risked heading back out to search for his family."

"So his story about going to the bathroom in the woods…"

"Might have been the truth. He did have cholera at one point, don't forget. And no matter how hard we tried, we never were able to extract a confession or any actionable intelligence from the man. By the end of this, we may owe him an apology."

"He was waterboarded, Colonel."

John stopped, his hands balled into fists. "Don't you think that I know that? We didn't set out to torture an innocent man, it just happened. He was in the wrong place at the wrong time. But we won't know for sure until we speak with Ray."

They reached a long corridor packed with military personnel. Among them were General Brooks and Colonel Higgs, who were about to head into the dark room to watch the interrogation through the two-way mirror. Suddenly, a seemingly inconsequential piece of the puzzle took on a whole new meaning. John remembered how vehemently Ray had objected to Huan's torture. At the time John had attributed it to the man's kind and somewhat naive disposition. But now he could see Ray had been trying to protect Huan, perhaps on orders from his Chinese handler.

"You're back," Brooks said, about to head inside.

"Yes, and I heard about Ray. Let me be the first one to speak with him."

"John, I don't think that's such a great—"

"He trusts me, General. I hired him for the job. If I don't get anywhere then by all means send in the hounds."

Brooks glanced over at Higgs, who raised an eyebrow.

"First we'll need to fill you in on what we know."

"So I can speak with him?"

"You can," Brooks replied. "But you'll have five minutes."

•••

Following a quick debriefing, John took a deep breath and entered the interrogation room. Inside, Ray Gruber was still in his pajamas, his hands cuffed to the arms of his chair.

The cuffs made a metallic clank as he struggled to raise himself up. "John, there's been a terrible mistake—"

"Save the theatrics, Ray. I know everything. I'm not here to hear you plead your innocence. We're already past that point. First thing I wanna know is why."

Ray's eyes fell and the seconds ticked away.

"I want a lawyer."

John laughed. "There aren't any lawyers anymore. Probably the best thing to come from the social breakdown. It's just you and me, Ray. You, me and the truth."

"We aren't going to win this war, John," Ray said flatly. "No matter how much I tried to lie to myself, the writing was on the wall. I was just honest enough to plan ahead."

"For the Communist takeover?"

"You're what they used to call a survivalist, John. You know, do whatever you must to stay alive. Well, what I did was no different."

John leaned back in his own chair. "I always took you for a naive optimist, not a pessimist and especially not a traitor."

"Guess it depends which end of the barrel you're looking down. I know what goes on in those camps and I sure as hell wasn't going to be dressed in rags with a number tattooed on my arm."

"And what about now? You're a tired old man in a pair of pajamas. How'd that plan work out for you, Ray?" John folded his arms. "What did they promise you?"

Ray stared down at his hands. "The one thing you couldn't. A comfortable life once this mess was over and done with. I just wanted things to go back to the way they were before, John. Was that so wrong? Right now we're nothing but a wounded animal that needs to be put out of its misery. It was the only humane thing to do."

"By selling your country out to the Chinese? Geez, Ray, if you'd told me you did it for a boatload of money or a harem of young girls maybe I could see it in you."

"It's about being on the winning side, John. And when they finally roll in here and take everyone you've ever loved? What will you have then?"

"My dignity, Ray. I'll have my dignity and the knowledge that when the going got tough, I still had my faith. It's easy to give up. Trust me, I know. After Iraq I was three-quarters of the way there, but I didn't check the odds, I fought back and with everything I had."

Both men sat staring at one another.

John was the first to break the silence. "They're gonna kill you, Ray. And it won't be a quick one either."

Ray winced.

"I'm not trying to scare you. I'm just shooting straight. Unless you can give me a reason to spare your life, and it better be a darn good reason, even I won't be able to help you out of this one."

Ray scanned the room, searching every nook and cranny, perhaps for a way out.

"Do they know?" John asked.

"Who?"

"The Chinese. Do they know you've been made?"

Ray shook his head.

"What about other agents?"

"In Oneida? There aren't any."

"You sure? What about David?"

"The kid's innocent," Ray said with disgust. "His only crime was pulling his pants down in the forest to do his business. People latched onto him so tight, he had me convinced I would never get caught. He was a scapegoat, nothing else."

Another pause as John let Ray's new reality sink in a little.

"You got some good men killed. That's something I'll never forgive you for. But you've got a chance to work for us now, Ray, and maybe, just maybe you can start making amends for what you've done." John stood and walked to the door. "So, Phoenix. What'll it be? Will you work for us now or should we start measuring the hangman's rope?"

Ray's eyes stayed glued to the table and suddenly John could see he was no longer looking at a captured Chinese agent, he was watching an old man who'd sold his soul to the devil, one who wasn't sure if he would ever get it back.

Ray spoke, his voice barely a whisper. "I'm in."

Chapter 51

"I think it's time we set David Newbury free," John told General Brooks and Colonel Higgs. The three men were in the dark room watching a deflated Ray Gruber through the two-way mirror.

"We've already seen to that," Brooks replied. "But he can't stay in Oneida, not anymore. In the minds of a lot of folks here, he's still guilty."

"We sure did jump to conclusions," John admitted. "We learned an important lesson here. Knowing there's a mole in your midst has a nasty habit of making the best of us paranoid. I'm just sorry David had to be the one to suffer for that."

General Brooks opened a file and tossed it on the table in front of John.

"What's this?"

"A report from the front lines," Higgs informed him. "Seems the Chinese have redeployed a sizeable portion of their forces to meet the NATO threat from the north."

"So Ray already sent it in?"

Brooks flipped the page. "He did, along with info on the planned mission to blow up a trainload of supplies that never existed."

"I had a feeling," John said, unable to stop seeing the faces of the three men he'd just lost. "I guess that's what counter-espionage is all about, right? Lie to your friends and hope the information somehow makes its way back to the enemy."

Brooks handed John another folder, this one with the words TOP SECRET stamped across the top in red letters. Inside was the outline for an operation called Anvil. It looked like a full-out assault on the Chinese forces camped along the foothills of the Appalachians. Listed among the American and allied forces were ten divisions of NATO troops. But they weren't coming in from the north, as the Chinese believed. The landing in Halifax had been one of those little fibs John had alluded to earlier. It wasn't a complete lie, of course. A single division had come ashore and was pushing south. The Chinese had to believe some sort of relief force had arrived. The main landing, however, had come through the port of Norfolk nearly a week ago, and most of the men and materiel were being sent to reinforce the American center in preparation for the main thrust.

John shook his head.

Both General Brooks and Higgs looked on in surprise.

"You finally got your offensive, John." Brooks paused. "I thought you'd be more pleased."

"The Chinese are dug in all along the line," John told them. "There's too much that can go wrong launching a frontal attack."

"Yes, but our side's been stockpiling ammunition and fuel for one giant push," Brooks countered.

"I'm sure they have, and so did Hitler in the winter of 1944 when he threw everything he had against the Allies. As you surely know, they had limited fuel for their Panzers, which meant that if the Germans didn't seize fuel depots soon enough, the entire advance would grind to a halt."

"We don't need another history lesson, John," Brooks shot back. "I'm showing you this plan out of courtesy, not to get your okay."

"I appreciate that, General. I just think there's a

better way."

Brooks sighed and grabbed the folder back.

"It can't hurt to hear him out," Higgs said.

Brooks was seated now, looking like a child who hadn't gotten his way.

"Those who fail to learn from history…" John began.

"Are bound to repeat it," Brooks said impatiently. "Yes, we know. What is your suggestion?"

John glanced through the two-way mirror at Ray Gruber. "I say we used the one asset the Chinese will never suspect. First we get Phoenix to feed the enemy false intel that our troops are starving and deserting every day by the thousands and that our center line is on the verge of collapse. With the threat of a large NATO relief army bearing down on them from the North, the Chinese supreme commander might realize it's now or never and throw everything he has right at the American center. Then we do to the Chinese what the Carthaginians under Hannibal did to the Romans at the battle of Cannae."

"We pull our men back in the center, feigning a rout," Higgs said.

"Precisely. We draw the Chinese in until they're fully committed and then we swing our flanks in and snap the trap shut." John pushed his hands out and then clapped them together to emphasise his point.

"But what about the NATO forces?" Brooks asked, perking up in his chair.

"When the Chinese realize they're being surrounded," John told them, "that's when NATO pushes up through the center and annihilates what's trapped in the pocket."

"Well, I'll run it by General Dempsey, Colonel Mack, but I can't promise you he'll go for it."

"Then tell him it was your idea."

Brooks looked up, surprised. "It's your plan," the general said. "You deserve the credit or the reproach."

"I don't care for either one," John replied without flinching. "If I had it my way, I'd be back at my cabin, clearing a patch of land so I could start growing some simple crops."

Colonel Higgs smiled. "You're the last of a dying breed, John. A true citizen soldier."

Higgs was talking about the tradition during the Roman Republic of soldiers who would hang up their weapons and armor after the conclusion of a campaign in order to return to the family farm.

From inside the interrogation room, Ray began calling John's name.

"John, if you can hear me, there's something important you might wanna know. It's about Brandon."

Chapter 52

"Tell me you know where he is," John said, slamming the interrogation room door behind him.

Ray sat up straight. The man's face was flat, as though he no longer felt the need to lay on the charm.

"Of course I know," he replied, his cuffs rattling against the arms of the chair. "His unit's been moved to Jamestown."

John's brow furrowed. "Tennessee?"

Ray nodded. "That's right. All you need to do is head through the Scott State Forest. But I'm not the only one who knows, John. You and your Rough Riders have become something of an itch in the Communists' backside. A Chinese special ops team's been tasked with taking you and your men out."

"The ambush near Lenoir City," John said. "That was them."

"They wanted me to handle it myself, but I told them getting close to you wasn't so easy."

"You lied."

Ray frowned. "You may not think much of me, John, but I also have my limits. Although I'll admit those limits didn't involve withholding from the Chinese that Brandon was your son."

"My son? You told them that? But it isn't true."

"Sure it is, John. Diane might not have given birth to the kid, but you've treated him like a son since I've known you. Gregory felt it too. Why do you think he was so desperate to make you proud of him?"

"I don't need a lecture from you."

"No, you don't. And mainly because you don't have time. That special ops team is under a man named Zhang Shuhong, one of the most ruthless commanders they've got. He and his team are heading for Jamestown as we speak. I handed you to them on a silver platter and they failed, so now it seems the plan is to lure you out into the open by threatening the life of someone you love."

"Why are you telling me this? So you can spring another trap?"

"No, John. To show you that I can be trusted."

•••

As soon as John left he was intercepted by General Brooks.

"The new battle plan is a go, Colonel Mack."

"You pitched it to General Dempsey?"

"I did and he loved it. Although I decided to follow your advice and claim the idea as my own.

John grinned.

"But there's a catch."

"Isn't there always."

"All available forces in Oneida have been redeployed to a town near the Appalachians called Colonial Heights. It overlooks the junction of Interstates 81 and 26. And it'll be our job to ensure the trap we've set stays closed. That means stopping any Chinese troops attempting to flee. So start getting your forces together. Whatever militia Oneida can spare will need to head out by first light." General Brooks collected the files on the desk. "I heard your conversation with Gruber, John. I'm sorry, but there isn't time for a mission to save Brandon right now."

"But General—"

"That's an order."

John gritted his teeth. "Yes, sir."

By the time John left the jail, the crowd out front had largely dissipated. Already preparations to move out were underway as Humvees sped through the cleared back streets, some towing 155mm artillery pieces.

Back at the radio room, he caught up with Henry.

"I need you to reach out to your contacts in the resistance," John told him. "Something big is going down. I want ambushes set up along every major highway and interstate heading east. At some point within the next twenty-four hours the Chinese are gonna try to send reinforcements to the front. We can't allow that to happen."

Henry's eyes were wide.

John turned to leave.

"Where are you going?"

John paused without looking back. "To save one of my sons."

•••

Not long after, John secretly set out with the rest of Alpha squad, heading for Jamestown. In the earliest days of the struggle, the town had been one of the first liberated from the Russian fifth columnists sent to take over. Then the Chinese had showed up, causing many of the folks to flee, heading through the Scott State Forest to join those already in Oneida.

For once, John's plan was simple. He didn't have one. The group of eight men—Heller would have made nine—made quick progress on horseback through the narrow forest trails. He supposed for disobeying a direct order, he risked court martial and maybe even execution, but it was a risk worth taking. The men accompanying him didn't know any better, but that would only help to solidify their innocence.

A sparse collection of small homes on big plots of land signaled the outskirts of Jamestown. These would help to provide some cover for John and his men as they drew closer to the military barracks located further into town. With little to no intel, they would need to hunker down somewhere with a good vantage point and observe the comings and goings.

An abandoned barn nearby offered as good a place as any to keep the horses. The rest of their weapons, along with the M30 mortar and the M249 wielded by Benson, would be carried on their backs the old-fashioned way. As had become the norm, Reese split from the group, heading south to do some reconnaissance, armed this time with the suppressed Remington 700.

The truth of the matter was, they hadn't come here with the sole aim of freeing Brandon. He was only one of several Americans press-ganged into serving in the Chinese army. Chances were good that each of them had been told if they failed to perform, their family members back at camp would be executed on the spot. As the special forces commander seemed to understand well enough, if you wanted to manipulate the man, your best bet was to threaten his family.

The remaining seven men from Alpha broke into two teams. One team of three—John, Moss and Benson—would make their way onto a nearby rooftop and try to identify which building was being used as the barracks. The final team of four would carry the mortar and head north.

Moss pointed to a cell tower. "If you can handle

heights, that's probably our best bet."

They made their way up the tower, leaving Benson and his M249 at the base pulling security. Near the top, John felt a strong wind trying to push him over. He held on with one hand and brought his binoculars up with the other.

"See anything, boss?"

"Not a whole lot," John said. "Town seems emp… wait a minute. I got a group of four soldiers heading down the main thoroughfare."

"A patrol?"

"Looks that way."

"At least now we know someone's home." John paused. "Two, maybe three Caucasians. But it's hard to be sure."

"Colonel, come in," Reese squawked over the walkie.

"Go ahead."

"I've got eyes on a Wal-Mart west of your position with lots of activity. I've counted at least two dozen soldiers coming and going."

"Are they carrying anything?" John asked.

"Only their weapons. I'd say a number of 'em are Americans too, over."

"So you think that's the barracks?" Moss asked.

"That's my guess, and probably the local headquarters too."

John spoke into the walkie. "Reese, stay put and keep your eyes on that front entrance."

"Hold up, Colonel," Reese said at once. "Eight to ten spooks in black fatigues just entered the store."

"Same boys who hit us near Knoxville?"

"Hard to say," Reese replied. "But they sure are dressed the same."

"Okay, keep eyes on. We're moving around front to support you."

John then ordered two members of the team to the

north to redeploy atop a hill about three hundred yards from the store. The other two were to cover the exit around back. That way anyone coming or going would be under fire.

"Any ideas?" Reese asked once they'd climbed down and redeployed. One by one, his men radioed that they were in position.

John felt that familiar twitch in his belly. "I was hoping you'd have a suggestion."

"I appreciate your confidence, Colonel. We can always employ the old pheasant-hunting tactic."

"Enlighten me," John said, intrigued.

"A sniper trick used by the Russians in Stalingrad. They'd identify a German command post, send in a few mortars in to loosen things up and when the German commander and his lieutenants came scrambling out, they'd drop 'em dead."

"The rest of you get that?" John asked the team.

They replied in the affirmative.

"But watch your fire. I wanna do everything we can to avoid American casualties. Your main targets are the special ops troops in black camo and the People's Liberation Army soldiers. Leave the Americans to me."

And with that John called in three high explosive rounds on top of the store.

The first round fell short about ten yards to the left, destroying four rusted hulks still in the parking lot. A black puff of smoke rose up from the impact site. Since the store was in visible range for the mortar team, they immediately adjusted their fire. Seconds later the next round struck the roof. The detonation echoed off the surrounding homes. A yellow and orange gout of flame rose up from the roof. Right away, a handful of Chinese troops came swarming out of the improvised barracks.

"I got tangos all kinds," Reese called out. "But it's hard to tell the Americans from the Chinese."

Two special forces soldiers emerged and John and Moss engaged them right away. Both dropped before they knew what hit them. But now the enemy could see where the rounds were coming from.

"Colonel, two more spooks just came out the back of the store," the rear team reported.

"Take them out," John shouted back.

The sound of gunfire erupted all around them.

Reese, positioned in the upstairs of an abandoned house, had knocked out a few panes of glass which he used as a loophole. He'd even positioned a filter screen to help mask his position. Even someone staring directly at his location would never know he was deep inside the room.

A muffled report from Reese's Remington sounded a second later, followed by another special ops soldier dropping in the parking lot.

"Send in two more mortar rounds," John called over the walkie. "Place these toward the back of the store. We wanna send them all out the front."

John used his binoculars, scanning over the small clusters of Chinese troops firing back at them from behind rusted cars in the parking lot. They had the sun in their eyes, which explained why many of the shots were zipping over the heads of Alpha team. That was when John spotted a group of Americans. Ten soldiers, huddled behind a row of shopping carts. Their weapons were at the low ready, but they weren't firing.

"I need to get closer," John told the others. "Cover me."

Before Moss could stop him, John high-crawled out from cover and worked his way toward the parking lot. The sound of AK rounds whizzing by pushed his head lower to the ground. He needed to get into shouting distance. By the time he reached the concrete the rate of fire coming toward them intensified. Some of the special forces were firing from their own concealed positions. The consistent thud from Reese's suppressed rifle reassured him his men were still firing back.

"Moss, call in some mortar rounds on that clump of trees at the other end of the parking lot. There's at least one spook back there."

"Aye, aye."

Just then came a loud crack as a sniper's bullet impacted the butt stock of John's AR. He rolled behind a clump of bushes.

"Reese, we may have a cuckoo on our hands," John called in over his walkie.

A cuckoo was military slang for a sniper in a tree. During the Second World War many snipers were left behind in this way to cover the retreat of German troops from Russia.

"Scanning," Reese called back.

Another shot hit the ground by John's right arm. Pinned down with nowhere to go, it was only a matter of seconds before the next shot finished him off.

Seconds stretched into hours before John caught the silenced report from Reese's rifle.

"Sniper down," Reese said. "You were right about finding him in a tree. Saw a dark shape in the leaves of a maple and let him have it."

With the enemy sniper out of action, John pushed himself up to his knees. The firefight was far from over and bullets were landing all around him. From behind him, Benson's M249 and Moss' M4 laid down an impressive volume of covering fire.

Cupping his hands around his mouth, John shouted, "American conscripts! The camp near Jonesboro has been liberated. There's nothing anyone can do to your families."

That was when the special forces commander, a red

star adorning his helmet, rolled out from behind a nearby car. In that instant, John realized with horror he wasn't going to have enough time to raise his AR to defend himself. Time slowed and the hatred and determination on the commander's face left John with the utter conviction he was about to be killed.

Both of his arms swung down by his right side. That was where his assault rifle dangled from a two-point sling. His muzzle was halfway to the target when the commander's chest exploded. For a moment, his eyes registered surprise and then frustration. There was no third emotion.

The remaining Chinese soldiers rose to flee and were cut down by the American conscripts.

John patted himself, searching for the wound he was sure he'd taken. Finding none, he breathed a deep sigh of relief and looked up to find a group of Americans in strange uniforms standing not ten feet away. Among them was Brandon.

Chapter 53

By the time the enemy was cleared out of Jamestown, they'd freed close to sixty American conscripts. The roads in and out of Oneida were still guarded by Chinese roadblocks and so John ordered them to return to town on the same trails through the Scott State Forest they'd used to arrive. The downside was that it would take the men a while to march the fifteen miles home, especially since he'd ordered them to carry as many extra weapons and as much ammo as they could. The rest of the supplies were strapped to the horses.

John left Reese and the other men from Alpha to accompany Brandon and the soldiers back to Oneida while he and Moss went ahead. They were on the cusp of launching a major offensive and preparing everyone on their individual missions and responsibilities would take time.

No sooner had they arrived at the stables in Oneida than a sergeant from the 101st informed them Brooks was looking for them and he wasn't happy. Of course, the soldier used a far more colorful metaphor involving boiling feces that created a rather vivid and disturbing image in John's mind.

"Moss, you stay behind and make sure the rest of the Rough Riders sort through their gear. I want everyone ready to go in two hours. And bring the entrenching gear. We'll likely be digging in the minute we arrive at Colonial Heights."

"I'm on it."

John rode his horse through the bustling streets of town. Around him was the ghostly squeal of M1A2 tanks and Bradleys heading through the town's back streets as they assembled to the east. There weren't nearly enough vehicles for the thousands who'd be joining them, so many of the infantry would need to head there on foot, a journey which would take many hours of hard marching. As it was, they would be coming up behind the Chinese position and the timing of their advance was critical. If they left before the enemy fell for the ruse and made a concerted push toward the American center line, they risked being caught out in the open and destroyed. If they waited too long, they might let the retreating Chinese escape. Of course everything would hinge on whether the enemy believed the false intel Phoenix was feeding them.

General Brooks was in the radio room when John arrived, pacing back and forth like a caged animal.

"I could have you court-martialed, Colonel," he shouted. "We're on the threshold of the biggest operation of the war and you go off disobeying a direct order."

John bowed his head. "I brought sixty more American troops as well as weapons and ammunition from Jamestown."

"I'm sure you did, but that doesn't change a thing. I should put Moss in charge of your outfit and keep you here under house arrest."

"If I didn't bring Brandon home, General, it wouldn't only have killed his mother and sister, it would have killed Gregory and likely the morale of many more.

The Marines never leave a man behind and neither should we. There's no excuse for disobeying a direct order and I'll accept my punishment."

"All right, John. You're lucky I need you. I don't care that this attack plan is your brain child, if you push me again, I won't hesitate."

"Understood."

The two men stood staring at one another.

Henry was on the radio and looked back, concerned.

"Did Phoenix send the Chinese the message?" John asked.

Brooks nodded. "A few hours ago."

"Any new troop developments?"

"Not yet."

"If they attack without warning, we might not make it in time to keep the pressure on," John said.

"Yes, but when do battles ever go according to plan? Getting there may be the least of our worries. We'll have the unknown and Murphy's law to contend with." Brooks glanced down at a piece of paper in his hand. "General Dempsey thinks you're some kind of Ulysses S. Grant. Frankly, I think you're overrated and more importantly, I don't think we have nearly enough men and materiel. There's over a million Chinese troops strung along that mountain range and maybe five thousand of us. I'm worried it's gonna be a bloodbath."

A signal came in then and Henry pressed the headphones close to his ears. A moment he turned back, his face ashen. "The Chinese have begun their attack."

Chapter 54

Diane and Emma were in the kitchen preparing lunch when John arrived and explained the situation.

"But who's going to stay behind to defend Oneida?" his wife asked.

"The garrison will be more smoke and mirrors than actual men. We'll set up machine-gun nests at key strong points, but most of the able-bodied men and women who know how to use a rifle will be marching east sometime within the next hour."

"If you hadn't suggested this plan in the first place," Diane scolded him, "none of you would be leaving."

The urge to crack a smile nearly got the better of him. "If you had a nickel for every time I told you you were right you'd be a rich woman. This plan is the best chance we have of saving American lives. General Dempsey was about to order a full-frontal attack on dug-in Chinese positions. The carnage would have been unbelievable."

"Yes, but do you need to risk your own life, John?"

"I don't want you to die, Dad," Emma said.

"Neither do I, believe me," he said, touching the back of his daughter's head. "But how can I possibly ask my men to charge into battle if I'm not willing to stand beside them? Our faith has carried us this far. Don't let it waver now when we need it the most."

They caught the sound of footsteps heading tentatively down the corridor toward them. Soon a figure appeared in the doorway, one Diane and Emma didn't recognize at first. Brandon dropped his duffel bag at his feet and smiled weakly and that was when Emma fainted.

•••

John held his daughter in his arms while Diane fanned her with cool air.

"I didn't mean to," Brandon said sheepishly.

"She's been hoping for this day for so long," John told him. "If Justin Speeber had walked through the door, she wouldn't have been more surprised."

"It's Justin Bieber, Dad," Emma said, coming to. "And I don't listen to him anymore."

John helped his daughter to her feet. "Hey, what do I know?"

She held onto the table as she stared at Brandon and poked him with her finger.

Diane snickered. "Yes, he's real."

"And I suggest you hug him quickly before he goes," John told her.

Emma looked physically wounded by the suggestion.

"I'm sorry, honey. We need everyone with combat experience we can scrape together."

"But, Dad, he just got back."

"I'll give you two a moment," John said. He turned to Brandon. "Be at the rendezvous point in thirty minutes."

Brandon nodded as Emma's eyes filled with hot tears. The thought of torturing her in this way was heartbreaking, but there was no other way around it. The boy would never admit it to Emma, but he wanted desperately to be part of the American counterattack. John only prayed he'd come home to her in one piece.

Chapter 55

As promised, within the hour, the column left Oneida. Nearly six thousand strong, the force consisted of the scattered units from the 101st, 278th, and the 3rd Infantry Division as well as members of the town militia. The decision was made that they would move as a group. The tanks and Bradleys were split evenly between the front and the rear. At the back were the Humvees, many of them towing the 155mm artillery that had served them so well during the Chinese assault on the town. Over the last few weeks they'd managed to scrounge up enough fuel for the vehicles to enable a one-way trip to Colonial Heights. Finding a ride home afterward was something they would need to figure out when the time came.

Up toward the front of the group were John and his Rough Riders. Since many of them were on horseback, they could scout ahead and keep an eye out for Chinese roadblocks or ambushes.

The noticeable lack of such contact was not sitting well with any of them. They'd expected a running battle as they broke through the ring of Chinese forces on the way to their objective. Instead, it felt more like they were on a Sunday stroll east along Interstate 81.

Moss and two others came riding up alongside John.

"We just came across a Chinese anti-tank battery set up as part of the siege of Oneida."

"Did you come under fire?" John asked.

"The gun wasn't real. It was just a few logs lashed

together and spray-painted green."

"Was the paint fresh?"

"It looked it," Moss said.

"The Chinese must have pulled men off the siege in the night to help bolster their offensive."

"You look worried."

"I only hope the Chinese attack doesn't somehow manage to break through. If they're gathering soldiers off a high-profile threat like Oneida, there's no telling how many of the enemy our boys in the mountains will be facing." The thought brought him back to tales he'd heard from the Korean War where US GIs described hordes of Chinese troops swarming over the hills like hungry locusts.

•••

Every once in a while they would stop in order to establish radio contact with General Dempsey's headquarters for a status report. The general himself was far too busy to speak with Henry or Rodriguez, but as John feared, one of his aides described a Chinese assault far more ferocious than any of them had expected. Over the last few weeks, each side had been sizing each other up like punch-drunk boxers. Crossing the Mississippi had been one thing, but dislodging a stubborn defender from hilltop positions was something else entirely.

It was only as they reached the edge of Colonial Heights, Tennessee that they came under fire. A platoon of Chinese soldiers were dug in along the interstate. Machine-gun nests with intersecting fields of fire would pose a problem for any approaching infantry. Immediately the armor moved up to eliminate the threat. The M1A2's power 120mm cannon shook the ground as it pounded the enemy positions from more than a mile away. After that the Bradleys moved in, a squad of infantry in each vehicle. They opened up with their 25mm M242 chain guns, tearing into the remaining strong points with lethal accuracy. Soon, the Chinese unit climbed out of their foxholes and ran for their lives.

On one side of the interstate stood a row of houses. On the other were industrial buildings with low, flat rooftops. Both offered the perfect place from which to set up an ambush. General Brooks came over the walkie on a channel reserved for commanders. "I want all of these buildings swept and cleared and defensive positions established within the hour. When those Chinese columns come rolling down the 81 looking for an escape route, I wanna make sure they get the greeting they deserve."

John and Moss shared a nervous glance. So far things were going smoothly. Maybe a little too smoothly.

•••

Since the retreating Chinese would be coming at them from east to west, the defensive lines were set up in a series of kill zones. Artillery and mortar teams on either side of the interstate zeroed in on both of the approaches. The 155mm howitzers would be loaded with DPICMs—Dual-Purpose Improved Conventional Munitions—an artillery shell loaded with smaller bomblets, each capable of taking out a tank. When the shell reached a specific altitude, it would explode, releasing the smaller submunitions. In addition, IEDs littered the northern and southern edges of the highway. Once the enemy got close, the detonations would isolate the tip where the Americans would get to work destroying them piecemeal.

As in Oneida, the second story of homes became

small fortresses unto themselves. Additional fire teams took position on the flat roofs of the industrial buildings on the southern side of the highway. They'd also brought what remained of the AT-4s, Javelin anti-tank missiles and Stinger surface-to-air shoulder-fired rockets. The latter was merely a precaution, for although the Chinese jets were likely shielded from the effects of the recent EMP, the supplies and replacement parts required to keep them in active service were not. This was why the skies over Oneida had been largely quiet and peaceful following the mission, save for Billy Ray's occasional barrel roll whenever he returned from a successful leaflet drop.

Banks of earth and sand piled up along the north and south edges of the highway had originally been designed to cut down some of the traffic noise, but the formation had inadvertently given the American forces a nice reverse slope they could use for defense. Rather than silhouetting themselves along the crest, a reverse slope defense allowed units to remain largely hidden from sight and protected from direct fire. Even indirect fire was blind since spotters couldn't observe the effects of the exploding shells.

In reserve, General Brooks kept a mix of his most experienced men, along with a couple hundred of his greener troops. Among the latter were Gregory and Brandon. For his part, John and his Rough Riders were also kept in reserve on the southern side of Interstate 81. The speed with which they could deploy allowed them to act as a quick reaction force, ready to apply fire wherever needed.

With everyone in position came arguably the most challenging part of any mission—waiting for the enemy to approach. If the situation at the front went well, then the retreating units heading their way would largely be shredded versions of their former selves.

John called Reese on the walkie. The sniper was perched in the tower of a nearby church. "You see anything?"

"No, sir. Just a long, boring stretch of highway in both directions. It's enough to get a man thinking. Once we're done with this mess, I'm gonna get me one of those motorhomes and head west."

John laughed. "Who knows, maybe Moss will join you."

"Oh, no, Colonel. I'm a lone wolf. Besides, I have some unfinished business out that way I've been itching to take care of."

"All right," John said. "Keep 'em peeled and lemme know as soon as you see anything."

"Roger that."

When they were quiet, they could hear the dim echo of distant battle.

"Sounds intense," Moss said, removing his magazine and blowing away imaginary dirt. "If it sounds this bad here, what's it like over there?" He paused and reinserted the magazine into his M-4. "You think this crazy plan of yours will work?"

John shrugged. "It's Brooks' plan now, not mine. And I hope so." He couldn't help thinking of Brandon and Gregory at that moment, both part of the reserve infantry formation, tasked with plugging holes and deploying wherever they were needed on the battlefield. Hopefully their nerves weren't getting the better of them.

John got on the walkie to Rodriguez. "Any update from the front?"

After a small delay, Rodriguez replied, "American

forces are pulling back as planned, but they're taking far more casualties than expected. The NATO force is still waiting to head into action, but they describe the situation right now as touch and go."

"That ain't good," Moss said with his usual talent for summing up a situation in three words or less.

A minute later Reese was back on the horn. "I got incoming."

John lifted the binoculars and scanned east along Interstate 81. There wasn't a soul in sight.

"You sure about that? I'm not seeing anything from where I am."

"Not east," Reese said, his voice betraying a slight tremble. "They're coming from the north, down Interstate 26. At least battalion strength—no, make that a division—and these guys aren't the Chinese."

John swung in the other direction and felt the blood drain from his face as he saw what Reese had meant. "God help us."

"I don't like the sound of that," Moss said, scrambling for a better look. "What do you see, John?"

John lowered the binoculars, his mouth suddenly bone dry. "The Russians are coming."

Chapter 56

The forward edge of the enemy advance was still about two miles north of where the interstates met when John radioed General Brooks and told him what was coming. Their own artillery was recessed a few miles from the front lines and could be called on at any time.

"An entire division?" Brooks asked. "Are you certain?" He'd been anxious to whip the retreating Chinese not long ago but he suddenly didn't sound so sure anymore.

"Positive," John said. "When you notify General Dempsey, tell him to send whatever support he can."

Brooks scoffed at the idea. The chances were slim the Americans along the main line had much help to offer. "Tell your men to stay hidden," the general advised him. "We've still got the element of surprise on our side."

A second later, the order went out. They would wait for the Russians to be drawn in before they sprang the trap.

Benson was next to John on the industrial roof and he racked his M249 and smiled. "Think we'll make it out of this one, Colonel?"

The corner of John's mouth turned up in a half-hearted grin. "Of course we will," he lied.

The others around them stayed low, prepared to spring when the signal was given.

Unexpectedly from the north came the telltale whoop of approaching helicopters.

"Reese, that what I think it is?"

The moments of silence ticked by with painful slowness. "Yes, sir," came the reply. "We got half a dozen Havocs closing fast."

Havoc was the NATO designation for the Russian Mil Mi-28 attack helicopter. An upgrade from the troop-carrying Hind made popular in so many movies, the Havoc looked more like the Apache and was just as deadly.

John switched channels, alerting the Stinger teams. The Americans' cover was about to be blown one way or another. It wasn't uncommon for ground forces to send air assets to scout ahead in order to avoid the very type of ambush awaiting them now.

John swore under his breath. They hadn't fired a single shot and already they were in serious trouble.

Seconds later the sound of the helicopters grew louder as small dots on the horizon grew in size. Painted in a green camo pattern, the choppers prepared to make a pass over the city of Colonial Heights when the first Stinger missiles streaked into the air, leaving white vapor trails in their wake. Since the choppers were flying low to the ground, there wasn't time for evasive maneuvers or to release flares to fool the incoming missile.

More missiles went up, exploding four of the six choppers in mid-air. Their flaming wreckage spun to the ground in slow circles, creating fireballs where they landed. The fifth chopper veered left, trying to flee, a newly fired rocket streaking up after it. The final Mi-28 fired its 30mm cannon wildly and managed to release flares as it too attempted to break contact. That was when a .50 caliber gun emplacement beneath it let loose. Sparks flew off the cockpit as it was riddled with fire. The helicopter made a lazy roll to the left and plummeted into a row of empty houses.

The main Russian formation was still over a mile away when many of the Americans rose up and cheered. One particularly boisterous bunch danced on the rooftop of a house on the northern side. Even the men along the embankment were giving each other high-fives.

"Get down and stop showboating," John shouted to their company commanders over the radio. "This isn't the Super Bowl."

He'd no sooner released the actuator on his walkie when that same house across the highway exploded into a giant fireball, instantly killing the men on the roof as well as the soldiers on the nearby embankment. John watched in horror as more bombs fell all along the line. They were getting bombed from the air, likely by Sukhoi Su-27 fighters, flying at altitudes beyond the range of the American Stingers. But without spotters on the ground, their bombs were falling blind, although the effect was still devastating.

"We gotta get off this roof," Moss said.

"And go where?" John replied. "One of those bombs hits this building, doesn't matter if you're on the roof or inside. You'll be lucky if they even need a spatula to pick up what's left of you. This is where we put our heads down and hope for the best."

"Colonel," Henry said over the walkie. "They've just taken out all of our artillery."

The air caught in his lungs. Catching the Russian armor in tight formation with a sustained barrage of cluster munitions would have been the difference between victory and defeat. John was no longer sure they'd be able to hold this position.

When John looked out with his binoculars, he saw the main body of the Russian advance had stopped about a mile away. A secondary element of what looked like TOS-1 mobile rocket launchers moved off to set up their own firing positions. Within a matter of minutes, this stretch of highway would be as heavily cratered as the surface of the moon.

Chapter 57

A dazzling explosion at least twenty thousand feet up in the air drew everyone's attention. The distinct roar of a fighter jet firing its afterburners was then followed by more explosions.

For a moment John wondered what was happening, until the new jets came screaming over the American position.

"They're ours," Moss cried. "F-22 Raptors. Man, look at them go."

And Moss was right in more ways than one. The bombs from overhead had stopped raining down on them, but it seemed their newfound guardians were moving off target just as quickly as they'd come.

John called Rodriguez at once.

"Compliments of General Dempsey, sir," Rodriguez told him.

"Yes, that's great," John barked. "But there's a huge column of tanks and rocket artillery about to tear us to shreds."

"They don't have the fuel, Colonel. I'm afraid it was all they could spare."

No sooner had John finished than Reese was on the line. "Russian armor's on the move."

"They're going to do a creeping barrage," John said.

Moss gave him a look. "A creeping what?"

"You pepper the enemy with artillery just ahead of your advancing units. That way there's a lot less of them to fire back at you."

"So is it time to find a good place to hunker down yet?"

John shook his head and pushed himself to his feet. "Negative. It's time for the last thing the Russians would ever expect. We're gonna go on the offensive."

•••

Within minutes, twenty members of the Rough Riders were on horseback at a full gallop, heading west along a depression of ground that ran parallel to I-81. They were armed with assault rifles, light machine guns and most important of all, AT-4 anti-tank rockets. They were about to do what guerrillas did best: sneak behind the front lines and strike the enemy where he least expected it.

On their right the metallic squeal of Russian armor pushing east toward the American position sent chills racing up John's legs, tightening his scalp. But it was those TOS-1s and their thirty multiple rocket launcher tubes that frightened him most. Only one BTR-T infantry fighting vehicle had peeled off to support them. That meant if John's men could get close enough to knock them out, it might just give the Americans a fighting chance.

He spotted the Russian artillery position on a small ridge, behind a clump of trees. The trees were meant to provide cover for the TOS-1s, but they also hid John's approach. The Rough Riders wheeled right, crossing the empty highway, and stopped to dismount thirty yards from the Russian vehicles. The horses' reins were all quickly lashed to the guard rail before the men moved to close with the enemy. John urged them on, reminding them their only chance lay in stopping those rockets from being fired.

As they reached the thin screen of trees, the soldiers with the AT-4s were ushered to the front. In the clearing beyond, John counted five TOS-1s. In front of them was a single BTR-T. He knew the fighting vehicle wasn't to be underestimated, since this particular model had been designed using the hard lessons the Russians had learned during the war in Chechnya. Thicker armor as well as a gun with a higher traverse meant enemies in an urban environment couldn't engage it as easily as its predecessors, the BTR-80 and BMP-2.

That was why he ordered two of his men with AT-4s to hit it first. The others would simultaneously strike the rocket artillery vehicles and thereby reduce the threat.

With his men quickly in place, John gave the hand signal to fire.

The first anti-tank rocket streaked out from the tube and impacted the turret of the BTR-T, knocking its main gun out of action. But the squad of Russian troops stormed out of the vehicle and dove to the ground, firing their weapons. John tapped Benson, his SAW gunner, on the helmet and Benson swung around, laying down an impressive volume of fire.

The other anti-tank rockets fired soon after and three of the five vehicles went up in a pillar of flame. The Russian infantry on their right were still pinned down, but a few had managed to toss hand grenades toward John's line, killing two of his men and possibly wounding a third.

That was when the two remaining TOS-1s fired their payload. The field filled with white acrid smoke and the deafening roar of rocket motors igniting. Suddenly everything disappeared from view. The men stopped shooting and only the sound of the wounded could be heard. Slowly the air cleared about a second before the rockets found their mark. Dozens of explosions rocked the American position.

The Rough Riders charged from the treeline, killing the remaining members of the Russian infantry squad and knocking out the two remaining TOS-1s.

"Reese," John shouted into his walkie. "Status report."

There was no response. He called again and waited before hearing a voice on the other end.

"Nearly bit the big one there, Colonel," Reese said. "Looks like part of the church is on fire."

"We tried, Reese. Really, we did. We just couldn't get them all in time."

The sight of Russian tanks in the distance engaging targets let John know not all the Americans were dead or wounded.

He tried to bring up Rodriguez and General Brooks at headquarters and faced a wall of static. His calls a moment later to Henry were more successful. They struggled to hear each other over the roar of weapons firing nearby.

"I'm trying to get through to General Brooks," John shouted. "Tell him we knocked those last TOS-1s out of action."

"I don't know how to tell you this," Henry said. "But the headquarters took a direct hit." The emotion in the radioman's voice was unmistakable. "General Brooks, Colonel Higgs and Rodriguez. They're all dead."

Chapter 58

John and the others raced back as quickly as they could. The death of the senior leadership was a terrible blow. It could lead to a panic or, worse, the American forces being routed from the field. But the other stark implication was that John was now in charge.

Thick towers of black smoke rose from craters where the missiles had impacted. Several of the structures lining the highway as well as the suburban dwellings to the north were ablaze. Galloping alongside Interstate 81, John could see the Russian armor battling ferociously against his men. Tracers streamed back and forth. A BTR-T lowered its ramp to offload a squad of troops right as an AT-4 streaked in through the hatch, blasting the vehicle into the air and killing everyone on board.

The handful of American tanks and Bradleys running and gunning from one concealed position to another didn't stand a chance. Seeing the burning hulks of American armor made John sick to his stomach.

Approaching the industrial building they'd been in before launching the attack on the TOS-1s, John saw that it had taken a direct hit and was on fire. He got on the walkie and called for the company commanders to report in. Slowly they came in, one by one, often little more than a quick reply amidst the sound of machine-gun fire. By the end, only fifty percent of the units called in. That didn't mean they were all dead, but it did mean issuing them orders would not be easy. He could only hope that their training and personal initiative would keep them alive and fighting.

The building next door hadn't been hit and John and his men climbed to the roof. Keeping low, they made their way to the edge where a platoon-sized group was already dug in along the edge, pouring fire on the enemy.

One of them was a Lieutenant from the 101st. "Sir, General Brooks is—"

"I know," John snapped, crawling next to him and taking aim with his AR. A group of Russian infantry were running behind one of the T-90s, taking fire from both sides of the highway. John looked for the squad leader and saw a soldier waving them forward. That would be his target. He squeezed off four rounds. The first two ricocheted off the rear of the tank and bounced harmlessly into the air. The next two found their target, dropping him to the ground. With the squad leader dead, the rest of the troops attempted to scatter and were immediately cut down.

"Russians are trying to flank the northern embankment by cutting through the suburbs," the lieutenant shouted. "If we don't do something they'll roll up our positions to the north and then do the same to us. What are your orders, sir?"

They were being overrun, plain and simple. Apart from attempting to retreat, there was no tactical decision that could win the day. What they needed was more help from the air. He got on the walkie to Henry. "I want you to find out what air assets we have nearby and patch me through to them."

Just as Henry acknowledged the order, the T-90 that had been trying to shield the infantry began swinging its gun turret in their direction.

"He's gonna fire on us," Moss shouted, getting up

and preparing to relocate. The others followed suit.

They hadn't gotten more than five feet before the Russian 125mm smooth-bore gun shot a round straight into the side of the building.

Shards of searing hot metal and chunks of cinderblock were thrown in every direction. Four men were killed outright, others lay wounded. John caught a scream ahead of him. Moss was lying on his back. A piece of shrapnel had taken his leg off below the knee. Blood gushed from the wound. With ringing ears and blurred vision, John scrambled on all fours to his friend. Reaching into one of his utility pouches, he came out with a tourniquet. Moss was still in shock and hadn't yet realized what had happened. He tried to stand up and fell back down.

John jumped on top of him, cinching the tourniquet above his wound. "Hold still, you stubborn mule, or you'll bleed to death." He applied a pressure bandage with blood-clotting chemicals and shouted for a medic.

John's walkie came to life. "Colonel, I'm putting you through to Major Donaldson."

"Major, this is Colonel Mack. We're in a real bad way here and could use a hand. A Russian armored division is about to break our position in half."

The walkie filled with static. "The Russians aren't supposed to be this far south."

"Yeah, well, tell that to them. We need all the close air support you can give us."

"Colonel, I've got an asset a few klicks from your position, but we're on strict orders to patrol our current location."

"Forget your orders, Major. The enemy is here. If you do as you're told, you'll be signing the death warrant for thousands of American troops. We're at the junction of Interstate 81 and 26. Our armor's been knocked out, so was our artillery, so whatever you see rolling on the ground belongs to the bad guys."

John didn't get a response.

The lieutenant from the 101st crawled up next to them, along with a medic, who took over.

"Are they sending anyone?" he asked, trying to mask the desperation in his voice.

"Doesn't look like it," John replied. "They've got orders to patrol an empty stretch of highway further east. I just don't understand it."

With Moss being cared for, John and the other unwounded soldiers made their way back to an intact corner of the building. The Russian tanks and IFV's were now drawing into two parallel columns, firing back at the Americans in both directions. AT-4 rockets streaked down from rooftops as well as the top of the embankment on both sides. A few vehicles were hit and exploded into violent balls of flame. Others were protected by their reactive armor and riddled the AT-4 teams with devastating fire.

A brave group of Russian troops stormed up the embankment, scaling its steep slope and engaging the Americans on the other side. John and the others fired down on them, drawing the attention of the armored column stretched along the highway. Heavy shells from the BTR's 30mm cannon ripped into their position and John ducked down, feeling the pebbles from the industrial roof hurled into his back and sides from the explosions.

A second later the BTR exploded in a yellow and orange burst of flame, followed by the T-90 right next to it. Soon the highway was awash with explosions that forced John's head back down for cover. It was only when he saw the Russian infantry melt under Gatling gun fire from the sky that he began to understand. Major Donaldson had sent an AC-130 Gunship, essentially a Hercules transport plane bristling with weapons. A

30mm Bushmaster 2 cannon, 105mm M102 Howitzer and ten AGM-176 Griffin air-to-surface missiles were only some of what the aircraft could bring to bear.

Overhead, it circled the battlefield, raining death upon the enemy with pinpoint precision. A company of Russian infantry that tried to take shelter under the overpass were obliterated by two shells from the Howitzer. The trail of fire flowed west along the entire Russian column. Soon the few support vehicles that were left turned and fled back north.

From there John took a deep breath and ordered his remaining troops to clear any remaining enemy troops from the suburbs.

"Major Donaldson gives you his best," the pilot said over John's walkie.

"Tell him when this is all over, I'm buying each one of you a beer."

The pilot laughed. "Roger that."

John scanned the air and saw the AC-130 head west, presumably back to base. He was about to give the order to move all the wounded into a makeshift triage area when Reese came over the walkie.

"I hope you're sitting down, Colonel."

"Reese, I'm glad to hear you're still alive."

"Not for long. I've got a line of Russian armor as far as the eye can see heading our way."

Chapter 59

John felt his entire world drop out from under him. "What?"

"Those Russkies who hit us just now, well, they musta been the forward tip of a much larger force." Reese paused and John could tell he was fishing in his pocket for what was likely his final cigarette. "Should we order a retreat?"

"How long do we have?"

"Hard to say. Maybe ten minutes before first contact."

He thought of Gregory and Brandon. Were they all right? His duties as a father and his duties as a commander pulled him in two competing directions.

A moment later Reese was back on the radio. "Colonel, I got a second massive formation heading in from the east."

The game was up. The Chinese were trying to break out of the American encirclement. Now it seemed it was John and his men's turn to be crushed between two irresistible hammer blows.

An orderly retreat was out of the question. The only hope for any of them at this point was to disperse and melt into the surrounding area. With any luck, at least some of them would make it back to Oneida. Or whatever would be left of it.

"Wait a minute," Reese said. "You may wanna hold that order."

"What do you see?"

"Those aren't the Chinese coming from the east. Those are our boys."

John found a better vantage point and scanned through his binoculars. But Reese was only partially right. What was approaching was the tip of the NATO spear. John swung to the left and saw that the Russian force was now about five miles away.

The sound of approaching aircraft filled the air. Flying low to the ground, a dozen A-10 Warthogs roared over them and John plugged his ears from the deafening noise. Close behind them was a group of Apache gunships. Thick clouds of black smoke soon appeared as the Russian column was torn to shreds. The carnage went on right up until the long line of NATO armored vehicles reached the interstate junction John and his men had been ordered to hold. He gave Moss a final check before he climbed down to greet them.

Many of the fighters who'd been defending the strip came out from cover, staggering toward the approaching troops as though part of a mirage. Many of the soldiers had bloody bandages wrapped over their heads or arms. Others had improvised, using pieces torn from their uniforms to stem a bleeding wound.

To the north, loud detonations continued as the Russian vehicles were devastated by American airpower.

John turned to the lieutenant. "Find out if my sons are all right, will you?" He didn't want to stumble onto what was left of them if the unthinkable had happened.

The lieutenant ran off just as a Humvee rolled up along the shoulder of the highway and pulled to a stop. Beside it, the long row of tanks and fighting vehicles continued to roll past, among them M1A2s, the British Challenger 2 and German Leopard 2.

The Humvee door swung open and an older officer in fatigues stepped out. John spotted five stars running down the center of his uniform and the name on his chest: Dempsey.

John and the others stiffened and saluted.

Cool and collected, Dempsey returned the gesture. "Where's General Brooks?"

John's eyes fell. "He didn't make it, sir. Neither did Colonel Higgs."

The general shook his head, scanning over John's shoulder to the sound of exploding enemy armor. "I can't tell you how sorry I am to hear that. I won't lie to you, Colonel, things were touch and go for a while back there. At first the Chinese refused to fully commit to the attack. Our center line must have been pushed back thirty miles before they were all in. If any of those Russian reinforcements had shown up, it would have tipped the scale in the enemy's favor. We owe you all a debt of gratitude."

Just then John's walkie came to life. "Colonel, the Russians are retreating."

Everyone present cheered, hugging each other, some shaking their weapons above their heads.

Hearing Reese's message must have made something click in the general's head. "Colonel Mack?" Dempsey asked, surprised.

"Yes, sir."

"I expected you to be taller."

John and the others around him smiled. "If I may," John replied, "I expected you to be younger."

Now they both laughed.

The armored column slowed to allow Brandon, Gregory and the lieutenant who found them to cross the highway. When he saw them, John fell on his knees and hugged them both.

"Are you hurt?"

They shook their heads. Gregory's hands were bandaged. "What happened?"

"One of the tanks near us was hit by a rocket and

Gregory ran in to pull the driver out," Brandon said.

John ruffled Gregory's hair.

"I did what anyone else would have done," his son said, trying to hide the surge of pride.

When they noticed General Dempsey standing before them they both stood at attention and saluted.

"At ease, soldiers. You did a fine job." Dempsey waved his hands over the men gathered before him. "I'm awarding each and every one of you a Silver Star."

"That's a great honor," John replied. "We do have quite a few wounded in need of attention."

"Yes, of course." Dempsey ordered his men to assemble the wounded and medics to care for them.

A squadron of F-22 Raptors roared over them as the soldiers below fanned out over the ravaged battlefield, searching for those in need of medical attention.

John was about to follow suit when General Dempsey pulled him aside.

"We intend to push them all the way back to the sea," Dempsey said. "You do realize that?"

"I expect our boys will chase them all the way home," John replied.

The general took John by the shoulders. "I could use someone like you, John. I know your rank was only intended to be a temporary measure, but I need someone with guts who can replace General Brooks."

"I'm humbled by the offer, sir," John began.

"But you're going to turn it down."

His hands fell to his sides. "I've served my country whenever she's asked me to."

"No need to explain, John. I understand. I'm only sorry you won't be there with us when we march through the streets of Beijing."

The two men saluted one last time and John was suddenly aware he was living through a historic moment, one he would tell his grandchildren about years from now.

Chapter 60

General Liang's headquarters at Berry Field near Nashville was in full panic mode. Officers rushed to destroy sensitive material in the face of the advancing Americans. Liang sat at his desk, smoking a Cuban cigar, a present from Fidel himself during a diplomatic trip to the island in the spring of 2007. The rich aroma and spiderwebs of white smoke filled the room.

His aide, Colonel Guo Fenghui, knocked briefly before entering. "Sir, the convoy leaves in ten minutes."

General Liang chopped at the smoke with his hand. "Can't you see I'm busy here?"

Guo stiffened at his superior's reproach. "If you stay behind you'll be captured."

"And if I return?" Liang countered. "What will happen to me then?"

Both men knew perfectly well what would happen. The Communist Party politburo would blame the failure on him, make him a convenient scapegoat and televise his public execution. No, this was not the thanks he'd expected for a lifetime of loyal service. They'd been double-crossed and hampered by a grassroots American resistance movement that required far more military assets than they could spare. They'd invaded an incredibly large country and, like Hitler's invasion of Russia during the Second World War, China's victory had depended on a lightning advance. One she'd failed to deliver.

"No, I will wait here and accept my fate without

flinching."

Colonel Guo's eyes flitted back and forth, as though he were searching for some way to convince the general to flee.

"Finish destroying those sensitive files and then I want you to leave," General Liang told him. "And that's an order."

Guo's eyes were red, his skin splotchy. "It was a pleasure to serve with you, sir."

Liang stood. "Likewise."

Guo saluted and then turned to leave.

"Colonel," Liang called after him. "Do not forget what became of Japan after she awoke the sleeping giant. One day soon the Americans will land on our shores. Promise me you'll be there to stop them when they do."

Colonel Guo promised he would and left.

When he was gone, General Liang finished his cigar, removed his Type 77 service pistol and put a bullet through his temple.

Chapter 61

Knoxville, fourteen days before EMP

John pulled up to James Wright's house and killed the engine. Exiting the vehicle, he tugged at the brim of his 278th ACR ball cap, stifling the urge to curse. Wright's front yard had become unrecognizable. The grass was knee high and in some places even higher. Weeds had pushed up through cracks in the driveway. There was no longer any mystery deciphering where Wright's property ended and his neighbor's began.

John wondered how many visits from the city he'd already received. No doubt Wright would not be a popular man in this neighborhood as long as his neglect continued to devalue the homes around him.

As his own life had slowly come back under control, John had come by several times in the previous weeks and James had never come to the door. Back then it was his wife Susan who had answered, usually with their youngest son Bradley cradled under her left arm. Even then the yard had begun showing signs of inattention and John had offered to mow the lawn, but Britany would have none of it. It was James' responsibility. If someone took that away from him, what reason would he have for getting out of bed in the morning?

As it was, James still hadn't managed to find a job. And that was part of the reason John was here now. His contracting business had started to pick up steam and it was time he began looking for some qualified subcontractors. Some of the properties John was working on needed painters and he knew James had done this kind of work before enlisting.

The mailbox by the front door overflowed with letters and bills. Those that didn't fit were piled in a small heap on the ground. John was beginning to wonder if the family had moved without telling him. Peering in through the living room window, he noticed that a light was on. He knocked nearly half a dozen times before James finally answered the door.

His army buddy didn't look well at all. He was wearing dirty briefs and a robe, stained with what John thought was peanut butter. Wright's long and tangled hair along with his heavy beard made him look more like a squatter than the owner.

"I was going to ask how you were doing," John began. "But I don't think I need to anymore."

Wright glanced over his shoulder, squinting at the light. His flesh was pale, nearly translucent, like a man who hadn't seen the sun in ages.

"I was just in the middle of some stuff," Wright said.

John nodded, not feeling the need to call out his friend's lie. "What about Britany and the kids? They around?"

A long pause as Wright brought the two ends of the bath robe together. "Gone."

"For good?"

Wright nodded, his eyes glazing over.

"You don't look like you've been sleeping well," John said, reaching down to collect the mail on the ground.

"Can you blame me?"

He handed the letters to Wright, who set them on an

even bigger pile next to the door. "I'm not here to blame you, James. I'm here because I'm your friend. You haven't been returning my phone calls. I've come by a bunch and each time all I see is your grass getting taller."

Wright looked past John at the miniature jungle growing on his front lawn. "Yeah, the phone got cut off." His eyes found John again. "What's your secret, John? You're always cool and under control. Never show a single crack."

"You couldn't be further from the truth there, James. I hit the bottom just like you. Hit it so hard I practically bounced and nearly lost everything I held dear. I dare say you might have gone one step further. But you know what made all the difference in the world?"

"What, John?" Wright said, his right hand coming out from behind the door, revealing a beer he'd been concealing. "The fact that you're so perfect that you never make a mistake?"

"Wrong there again. You're two for two, James. I fail more than I succeed. Not sure if you know that. Every victory is a battlefield littered with defeats. But the truth is, no one's counting. No one who matters anyway, 'cause it isn't how many times you lose, but whether you can pick yourself up off the ground."

"Is that why you came by, John, to gloat and shower me with your pearls of wisdom?"

John paused. "The truth is I came by because we're friends and friends help one another."

Wright was shaking his head.

"I also came by to offer you a job, James. And by the looks of things, you could really use one. But I didn't get back on my feet all alone. Not even Diane could help me with that. Judging by your current living conditions, we might be suffering from the same thing."

"Really? And what's that?"

"PTSD, James. Didn't even realize I had a problem

myself until I was too drunk to walk through my own front door. When your elderly neighbor and your wife have got you propped up, you know something isn't right. But it was the thought of losing my kids, imagining the crushed looks on their faces when Diane packed them up and left for good, that's what pushed me to start seeing a counsellor."

"Oh, I don't believe this," Wright began. "You come here feeding me this Sigmund Freud routine about how you started talking about your feelings. You're a coward, John. We're soldiers. That's what we were trained to do. Kill people. You go through a thousand military manuals and you'll probably never find the word kill, did you know that? The military's come up with a million ways to avoid saying the word, but when you boil it down, that's what we do. We're trained to take another man's life. Snuff it out without giving it a second thought. And if you're too weak to take that like a man, then you can step off my property and never come back."

John's chest was tight as Wright's hands clenched into fists, his face turning purple. He took a deep breath and spun on his heel to leave. Wright was still watching him, his chest heaving as John began to walk away. A second later John stopped and turned around. "A real man faces his demons head on," John said in a low voice. "The coward in me wanted to run and hide. Hide in a bottle of booze, hide by pushing everyone close to me away. Admitting I needed help and facing those dark memories was the toughest battle I've ever fought and I came a hair's breadth from losing."

The shift in Wright's eyes was subtle, but it was there.

"It's not too late to get it all back, James. Your wife, the kids, even this dump you call a house. You can have it again if you've got the guts to reach out and take an outstretched hand." John stood, staring at his friend for a moment before he turned to leave for good. Perhaps this was a lost cause. *You can't save people from themselves.* His mother used to tell him that and now he was beginning to understand how true those words were.

"I don't know, John. I see it's gotten you back on your feet, but I don't even have a car right now and…"

John dug into his pocket, produced the keys to his truck and rattled them in the air. "Don't worry. We'll go together."

Chapter 62

Three months after the battle

A thin layer of snow blanketed the top of Owens Ridge as John and Moss stood wrapped in warm parkas, chatting to one another. Behind them loomed the new Mack and Appleby family cabin, built with a helping hand from the entire community—a gesture of goodwill and appreciation.

"Mayor Moss," John said, letting the words roll off his tongue. "It has a nice ring to it, don't you think?"

"I think it's more responsibility than I thought it would be," Moss replied, and pulled up his pant leg to reveal his prosthetic leg. "And getting around on this thing isn't making it any easier."

John laughed, marvelling at how much about the man was different now. Even his trademark mohawk had disappeared in favor of a brush cut. "You're still wondering what to do about Ray Gruber, aren't you?"

"The council isn't sure whether he deserves a medal or a hangman's noose."

"A decision I don't envy them having to make," John admitted. "How's Henry doing as vice mayor?"

Moss blew in his cupped hands and jabbed them in his pockets. "I couldn't be happier with the choice. I'm glad he wasn't hurt that I'd asked Reese first."

"I'm sure he wasn't, but we all knew Reese would never stay."

"He found himself a motorhome and says he's

heading west. Has some personal business out there. But you're right, a guy like that can't stay in one place for too long." Moss kicked at a loose rock with his good foot. "I'm guessing you heard the latest from the front?"

John shook his head. "I've been too busy prepping for winter to think much about it. Brandon, Gregory and I have already chopped two cords of wood with plenty more ahead of us."

"We've broken through the enemy stronghold along the Rocky Mountains," Moss told him. "Some are saying come spring they'll be pushing all the way to the Pacific."

"And after that?" John asked, wondering where it would all end.

"Who knows? But there's already talk about electing General Dempsey president. He says his first order of business would be getting the lights back on."

As more and more American territory was liberated, communities all over had begun following Oneida's example and addressing their own power needs.

"I think Dempsey will make a fine president," John said, staring down at the town below them and the hundreds of residents working feverishly to get things back to the way they used to be. It would take time, but John was sure under Moss' watchful eye they would get there eventually.

The two men soon parted and John went around back to the small shed they'd built for George. The small structure even included a small wood-burning stove to keep him and his new companion warm through the cold winter months. John found Brandon and Gregory inside feeding them grass.

"Have you come up with a name for her yet?" he asked the boys.

A devilish grin appeared on Gregory's face. "I was thinking of Marilyn."

John couldn't hold back a burst of laughter. "As in Marilyn Monroe?"

"Yeah," Brandon said, tossing in a handful of grass. "Somehow those white feathers always make me think of that famous skirt scene."

Diane came up behind them, wrapped in a blanket. "Sounds like you boys are having too much fun out here."

"We were just discussing George and Marilyn," John told her.

"Marilyn?" She tilted her head. "They do look happy together, don't they? I wonder how long before we have a row of baby Georges to deal with."

John turned to Diane. "Where's Emma?"

"Inside."

"She still working on the war memorial?"

Diane nodded. "The town council voted to have it started in the spring and she wants to make sure it's perfect."

"Figures. She won't show it to me," John said. "Like it's top secret or something."

The boys both complained they hadn't seen it either.

"She's taking great care to get everything right, John. I've only seen some rough sketches, but it tells the entire story. It's quite stunning. You know that all she wants is for you to be proud of her."

"I am already," he said without reservation. "Of all my children. I hope each of you knows that."

Brandon and Gregory looked away, embarrassed, and John was glad that through all of the horror, they'd managed to retain at least some of their youthful innocence.

For many others, the EMP and the war that followed had stripped them of the very faith that made innocence possible. Faith in the government, faith in our fellow man and, for some, faith in a higher power. John couldn't help but feel that the country's struggle for survival had offered a unique opportunity for a fresh start, an opportunity to move away from political games and showboating and back toward the founding principles which had once made this nation great.

Diane wrapped an arm around him. "A penny for your thoughts?"

John smiled and kissed her gently. "That one's just for me."

Some Final Thoughts

Given that this is the final book in the Last Stand series, I felt it only right that I say a few words. Part of my goal in telling the Mack family story was to showcase how easily the safe and predictable world we know can be plunged into chaos. Spin a globe and press your finger down and it's likely to land on a country where danger, corruption and oppression are the norm. The savage realities of living in a city like Mogadishu, for example, might be foreign to many in the Western world, but I believe it's precisely the type of existence we'd face in the event of a massive social collapse.

And yet the amazing thing is that through all of that chaos and killing, it's still possible to find good, honest people who are willing to stick their necks out for others. In many of my email correspondences with readers this topic has often come up. It seems the prevailing prepper mentality nowadays is to shoot first and ask questions later when I think the opposite is what's needed most. Just as they say it takes a community to raise a child, I think it takes a tightly knit community to ensure a sustainable future.

I also wanted to provide a brief insight into how I approached the prepper tips in the books. Some have commented that after book two, the story stopped being about survival and became a military series. While this is true in part, each of the stories was designed to impart different kinds of survival lessons. Book one focused on urban survival. In book two the emphasis shifted toward outdoor tips. Book three examined how to fortify and defend a small town against a military attack, while book four looked at some of the considerations when operating an insurgency. Our soldiers fought insurgents in countries like Iraq, but God forbid, one day we may be forced to become insurgents ourselves.

If I haven't put you to sleep already, then I'll end with a confession. Between books three and four, I decided to take a small break and work on an altogether different kind of prepper story. Frankly, I wasn't sure fans of the Last Stand series would appreciate what I had written since it wasn't laced with prepper tips and featured a cast of rather colorful characters (without the colorful language, that is). As a result, I made the difficult decision of publishing it under a pen name. I'm sure many of you will spot the similar writing styles. All that is to say, if you're looking for something to pass the time as you wait for the next William Weber story, then this might be as good a place to start as any.

It's called *Long Road to Survival: The Prepper Series* and if you give it a shot, I hope you enjoy it just as much as you've enjoyed my other work.

Respectfully,
William H. Weber

Thank you for reading
Last Stand: Turning the Tide!

I'm always grateful for a review. Any thoughts, comments or feedback can be sent to my email:
williamhweberauthor@gmail.com

Find me on twitter (@Williamh_weber) where you can join my new release mailing list.

Made in the USA
San Bernardino, CA
09 April 2016